Necessary Sin

Brian W. Casey

For my wife Tina, whose constant support keeps me writing.

In Appreciation

Teresa Bryant

Lynda Smith

Michelle Ruth

Casey Nowakowski

Part One

What Goes Around

Present Day, Watercreek, Nebraska

Sheriff August Hawk walked over to the yellow tarp spread out off the road in the grass. Flashes of lightning lit the night casting blue light over the puddles formed in the valleys of the tarp mimicking the body underneath. Bending down on one knee, August pulled back the canvas.

It wasn't the woman he expected.

Even with the bruises and twisted disfigurement to the body from the wreck, August knew he was not looking at the woman he was to meet tomorrow. Her body was contorted like the dead deer he passed on daily patrols. Standing up and looking back at the responders August could read their lips. He knew what happened down below was spreading through their radios and whispers like a bunch of cackling women sitting around Trish's Beauty Shop on a Saturday morning.

Thirty-five years earlier, North Philadelphia

Francis Stratton connected with the ball. It nicked off Mrs. Roster's clothes line pole and into the waiting glove of Sister Alice Margaret. She was the boys' sixth-grade teacher and current first baseman. Francis thought about ramming her off the base but then remembered he still owed her homework. He slowed to a walk as he approached her.

"What's the matter Mr. Stratton. If I was a boy, you would'a run right over me. The problem with you city kids, you ain't got no guts."

The boys liked when she talked like that. Francis liked Sister. She was holy and tough. He would do anything she asked which usually meant out of the house before sun up to serve Mass.

As he ran back to home plate Francis spotted the mailman through the narrow walkway between the row houses. Today was the day the letter should come.

"Guys, see you in school. Sister, nice catch."

"Francis don't you forget you owe me a report yet."

Thumbs up from Francis as he turned the corner just in time to see the mailman step off the porch.

"Sorry Francis, nothing for you today."

Chapter 1

Amazon Jungle, Brazil

Two men squatted in the tall grass cover surrounding a jungle lake. There is a faint metal on metal slide then a click as a shell is loaded in the chamber of a handgun. Four men work their way to the right of the two men. Every eye is fixed on the naked couple swimming in the lake. They watched as the couple wrestled with each other and splash back and forth like a couple of kids. The leader signals the men to stay low and quiet. His prize was right in front of him and he doesn't want to miss this opportunity. The man came out of the lake and grabbed a towel to dry off. A few snickers escaped from the men on his little "manhood." They were more interested in seeing the woman do the same thing. The leader passed a stern look at the men close to him knowing their lust could blow the whole mission. He had too much was riding on this.

Chapter 2

Jack Stratton pried the lid off a can of sardines and tore open a tube of crackers pulled from a wooden box marked BOOKS. Still inside the box were little cakes he squired away without his wife Monica knowing. Jack had slowly been building up supplies for this day hoping to keep them secret from Monica and surprise her with a little picnic.

The Jesuit missionary in the village suggested this spot. Its canopy of trees over a hidden lake made it a perfect getaway spot. Surrounded by all the lush foliage and tropical birds flying everywhere, it was hard to remember the poverty and persecuted conditions they left behind in the village.

Monica splashed Jack from the edge of the lake forcing him to turn around. As she emerged from the lake he took in her dripping naked figure. Her white figure against the green of the lake gave her the appearance of a forest nymph in a fairytale. All she needed was gossamer wings to finish the picture.

Jack grabbed a rolled towel and tossed it to her as if he was throwing a football to their son Francis back in the states. With one hand she pulled it out of the air. She slicked her short-cropped hair back with her fingers then wrapped the towel around her waist leaving her boyish breast exposed. She adjusted the small wooden cross hanging around her neck by a thin leather strap, a gift from their son Francis. She gave the cross a soft kiss before she let it drop between her breasts.

As Monica walked up to Jack she spotted the picnic spread he arranged on the grass. This was the first time in years they could do anything special for their anniversary and for Jack to remember, made it even better. She reached for him to meet her halfway. When they met she dropped the towel and pulled him to the lake with her. Before they reached the edge of the lake, he threw his shorts and shirt back to the shore and joined her. Naked and embracing they sank underwater.

The men waiting in the grass moved closer.

Chapter 3

After another hour of swimming and soaking up their little bit of paradise, the two decided to dry off. Their time away from the village was limited and they didn't want to be this far away when nightfall came. Jack was beginning to get a little uncomfortable. He always imagined eyes looking back at him in the deep jungle. He'd heard stories of jungle animals stalking humans from the cover they knew best and leaping out at the right time. The Amazon jungle was no place to be without any kind of protection especially at nightfall. Monica could sense Jack's suspicion. Trying to get him to lighten up a little,

"Jack, come on. We're alone out here, there's nothing to worry about. Father said no one really knows about this place except him. Relax for once will you. If you're a nice boy, I'll take you for another swim and you know what that could lead to."

"You're right. It's just what I do, you ought to know that by now. Thank God I have you to keep me in line, I'd probably jump at every little noise." Jack popped the cork on the small bottle of champagne he bought the last time they were close to any real civilization. He passed the bottle to Monica.

"Sorry, no champagne glasses in the jungle."

She took a drink like she was chugging a bottle of beer and wiped her lips with the back of her hand like a teenage boy sneaking a gulp from a bottle. This was one of the many things Jack loved about her. One minute she could be all proper and the next let out a belch like a sailor.

"Jack, before we leave this place, let's write our letter to Francis. I want to tell him all about this while we can see it. I want him to know there is more in this jungle than poverty, drugs and bugs the size of airplanes."

Francis was staying with Monica's parents until they finished this last tour with the Peace Corps. They were proud of him. Unlike many eleven-year-olds, he understood their mission. They often commented there were few children who could make a life for themselves only seeing their parents a couple of times in the last year.

Monica's mother was close with Francis and made sure that he never forgot what his parents were doing and why. This lifestyle made Francis an independent boy for his age. His individuality was tempered by his deep religious convictions. Much of this was due to the influence of his grandmother and the nuns teaching him.

Francis was the boy who served Mass every morning before school and stopped in the church after school just to pay a visit. He was also the same kid that questioned the teachers and at times pushed their limits of patience. These habits didn't go unnoticed by the parish priest and more than once he dropped the hint to Francis that he ought to consider a life as a priest. Francis however had other desires. He wanted to see the world like his parents. He often told his grandmother he wanted the adventure of the prophets but not the responsibility of the apostles.

Monica started to pen the first lines of the letter,

"Dear Francis, Your father and I miss you so much. We have taken a day away from the village to have a little picnic and cool down around a lake in the jungle. The local Jesuit priest, Fr. Demetrius told us of this little hideaway. I hope you are behaving for your grandparents. They tell me you are doing well in school. The young children here are eager to learn just like you. When we get home..." The pen dropped away. The letter fell between her legs as the first attacker charged out of the surrounding thick cover.

Chapter 4

When the men came out of the heavy growth surrounding the clearing the Strattons had no chance of escape. Jack jumped up and stepped in front of Monica as one man rushed her. Another attacker slammed a fist deep in Jack's stomach, doubling him over. The blow was followed by a knee that caught Jack square in his jaw. Jack dropped to the ground gasping for air as he watched two men grab Monica and bend her arms behind her back. Jack managed to get to his knees only to be kicked back down by one who appeared to be the leader of the group.

The man was giving others orders in a dialect not common to the people of the local village. Jack didn't need to understand the words to know the orders being issued to the other men. Two men pulled Jack to his feet. Blood filled his mouth from loosened teeth. One eye was swelling shut from the repeated blows. One of the men pulled Jack's arms tight behind him and bound them together with twine. Jack could feel his hands turning cold. Another kick in the gut sent him to the ground. Landing on his side he struggled to at least get back to his knees.

Jack watched Monica dragged by her arms behind her back. It wouldn't be long before her arms either broke or separated from her shoulders. Monica was crying for Jack which only made the attackers laugh and mock her. The leader picked up the half-finished letter and stuffed it in his shirt acting like he found a treasure map. The same man reached for the wooden cross around Monica's neck. He fumbled with the cross then began to laugh letting it fall back on her neck.

As the band of attackers started to leave the clearing with Monica, Jack made one last effort to get to his feet and charged towards them. A shot ripped through the tall grass.

Chapter 5

The bullet found a home in Jack's side. The force of the shot pushed him off his feet striking his head on a rock at the edge of the pond. Jack laid unconscious, his head dangling backwards submerged up to his nose. It was only when a bird landed in the water and sent ripples did the water lap up to his nose and shake him conscious.

Jack didn't feel the pain in his side right away. For a brief period, he didn't even remember he was in a jungle. Then the pain bent him in half. His hands throbbing behind him, gut burning and one eye all but gone he gave in and passed out again on the bank of the lake.

When he came to, he had a little more sense what needed done. Rolling, he reached the tall soft grass. Not sure what he was doing, working only by feel, he pulled long stems out, ripped them in half behind his back. Grabbing a handful of the shredded grass he rolled back to the muddiest portion of the pond and shoved the grass in the mud behind his back. Resting for a minute to gain some strength, he rolled back over the same spot with his stomach pressing his side against the mud and grass patch. Rolling back around to his back, the mud patch came with him and stopped the bleeding.

There was little feeling in his hands. He knew his jaw was broken judging from the pain he was experiencing when he tried to open his mouth. He was barely hanging on himself and knew Monica was not nearly as strong as he was. She couldn't last long. He had to find her.

Jack lost even more hope when he was finally able to get to the jeep they drove to the lake. The attackers flattened all the tires and the steering wheel was broken off. Even if he was in good condition it would take hours for him to walk back to the village. In his current state he would be lucky if he even made it back at all

Chapter 6

Monica's arms were limp from the torture they endured. No longer bound behind her, now they hung useless at her side like arms on a rag doll. Both arms ripped from their sockets they moved only by gravity. Pain shot through her with each little twitch.

The attackers continued to question her. She still had no idea what they were asking. They passed the letter picked up by the leader back and forth acting like it was their ticket to wealth and fame. It was obvious they had no idea what it said. Monica tried to keep the image of Francis in her head, happy and safe with her parents in Pennsylvania.

She was sure Jack was dead. She saw the last man of the band, turn and shoot towards Jack and didn't hear Jack call out for her after the shot. She was alive and planned to stay that way for Francis. Somehow, she had to survive.

The leader came over to her and put his face beside hers. She could smell liquor on his breath. He slid a large knife around her open collared shirt. He let the weight of the knife point stick in the hollow of her shoulders. Monica felt herself start to lose consciousness as he pushed deeper with the knife on her already screaming shoulders. She had no way of understanding what he wanted or explaining she was not who he thought she was.

Jack and Monica were warned some of the villages saw them as government agents sent to spy and stop the prospering drug channels which supported many of them.

The leader pulled Monica to her feet by the belt loops of her jeans and forced her to continue walking beside him. They were now in the second day of walking, never exposing themselves to any clearing. It didn't matter anyway, no one would be missing them and only a few of the village children might question their parents where their teachers were. Everyone would be too afraid of these men to go against them and start looking for two whites.

Chapter 7

Jack fell again. This time, he fell forward on his face. He could taste the warm saltiness of blood in his mouth. He was getting accustomed with the pain, he barely felt the aching from the fall. He had no idea if Monica was still alive, but he had to believe she was. The attackers didn't know he was alive. That was his only advantage.

Jack knew the next move might use all his available strength. Rolling up on his knees, he bent his arms as low as he could behind him. Sliding them down over his butt he pulled with his leg muscles, flexible from years of running, and slipped his body through the hoop formed by his bound arms. With his hands in front of him, he could now walk with better balance and focus on how to free his hands. Jack began looking for a rock along a stream bed that might work to cut the twine and free his hands.

Chapter 8

Monica could see in the distance what looked like an encampment. Olive green tents of various sizes circled around one central tent. An antenna poking out of the main tent reached up through a clearing in the canopy of trees. The low-pitched drone of a generator could be heard. As the group moved closer to the tents, Monica heard voices. She couldn't make out what they were saying but from their excitement they obviously spotted the men holding her coming through the dense growth.

The leader of the group ordered the rest of the band to go up to the tents. He stayed behind with Monica. As the other men moved forward, he increased his grip around her arm. She could feel the tension in his clutch as he moved the two of them out of sight of the tents.

With no warning, the sound of automatic gunfire cut through the air. A rush of birds hollered and took flight. Monica's captor pushed her body to the thick growth of the jungle floor protecting her like a prize. One man of the original band came running back in their direction. The leader and Monica, hiding in thick cover, watched as the man passed them. Once passed the leader broke from cover and raised a gun from his waistband, aimed at the runners back and dropped him with one ear ringing shot. Then the leader stood up in plain view of the men in the clearing as they shouted and waved for him to come forward.

Keeping his grip tight on Monica, he dragged her to her feet causing her to roll over, stumble and land on her back on top of her arms. The pain of a wrist snapping made her scream out and lose all control of her bladder. The man muttered something to her, clearly disgusted with her. The leader grabbed her by her waist, lifted her over his shoulder the way she saw men carry bananas and carried her the rest of the way to the tents.

Chapter 9

Jack found a rock to work on the cord restraints around his wrists. With one final hard scrape the binding broke loose. Unraveling the rest of the twine he rubbed his hands trying to push life into them. He could feel the blood moving to his fingers as his hands began to swell in pain from the rush of blood.

Jack rolled into the stream and felt the cool water soak through his clothes bringing with it a charge of energy he thought lost. He stood up in the middle of the stream and looked down on his reflection in the water.

Out of the stream he oriented himself back to the direction he thought the band of men headed with Monica. The trail was getting weaker as the matted grass he was following was springing back. Close to the end of the second day of walking Jack could see in the distance a clearing with tents and a lot of activity. Jack figured it was either the men he was tracking or a mining party surveying this region.

As Jack stumbled closer to the tents, he moved with more caution deciding to wait till night fall to move any closer. Jack found a spot away from the trail and closed his eyes for some needed sleep.

Chapter 10

When Monica and her handler stepped into the encampment the men greeted her captor like a returning hero. She looked at the bodies of the men who had been part of the raid laying in a pile next to the makings of a bonfire. The smell of diesel fuel coming from the pile of bodies confirmed what was planned. The new gang led Monica and her abductor into the large tent in the center of the encampment.

Inside the tent a radio was manned by a young boy she recognized from the village. The man holding her released her to another man who gripped her arm even tighter. The leader walked over to the young boy and ordered the boy to do something on the radio. The boy looked back at Monica. Their eyes met in instant recognition. He bent his head low away from her eyes. Whatever the boy did on the radio brought an instant response back. The words angered the leader and he slapped the boy across the back of his head, knocking him off his chair. The man went into a rage kicking whatever was close and pounding his fist on every flat surface. He charged over to Monica and grabbed her face with one hand and for the first time spoke to her in poor English. "You are a very unlucky woman."

What he said after that was lost on Monica as he reverted to the dialect she couldn't understand. He pointed an angry finger at two men sitting in the corner cleaning rifles. Jumping to their feet they ran over grabbed Monica from the man assigned to hold her and took her outside of the tent. The moon came out while they were inside the tent. The whole encampment was lit by the suspended nightlight.

Chapter 11

Jack woke staring into a bright moon that lit up the jungle around him. He could smell a cooking fire coming from the encampment. The thought of food made his stomach tighten. He struggled to stand, his legs and arms stiff from their rest. Once upright, Jack started cautiously towards the tents. Not needing to watch the trail as before, he looked forward rather than down. His lack of caution caught up with him.

In only a few steps he tripped over what he thought was a downed limb. When he looked at his feet, there was a body. The person was bleeding from a wound in the back. Jack crawled back over to the body, rolled it over and could see by the moonlight that he was one of the men who first attacked them. Jack searched over the man for anything that might help him understand who these people were.

He found a handgun stuck in the man's waistband. Jack pulled the gun, not knowing exactly how to use it but stuck it in his own waistband hoping it was ready to fire. Finding the body, Jack knew he was dealing with men who would kill even their own.

He hoped he was not too late for Monica.

Chapter 12

The new handlers seemed to have more compassion for Monica. One pulling a stained rag from his pocket, tried his best to splint her wrist with a stick. The pain while he moved it dropped her to her knees and he followed her down to the ground sympathizing with her pain. The other man found a canteen and offered her a drink which she drank with enthusiasm while he held it to her lips.

They moved her to a tent just opposite of the main tent. Inside the tent was a cot and blanket. The moon filtered through the green canvas of the tent giving the inside a ghostly glow. For the first time in two days, she was alone and not being gripped by someone. She was happy that Jack was dead and did not have to endure this same torture. She thought of Francis, and tried to picture him with her parents, free of any danger.

Chapter 13

Walking towards the encampment Jack felt a little braver with the handgun stuck in his waistband. The wound in his side was oozing from infection and he was feeling the fever through his body. His only hope was that he could hold on and find Monica. After that, he figured there would be little time left for him.

Jack made his way to the edge of the camp. He laid down in the jungle cover just beyond the clearing hoping that he would have enough strength to get back up when the time came. He could see a pile of bodies and tried to focus hard on the pile to make sure Monica was not part of it. Satisfied that she wasn't he lowered himself closer to the ground.

It wasn't long when the man who led the attack stepped out of the main tent. He was dragging a young boy with him. Only a few days ago the same boy was in Jack's reading class in the village. The man pushed the boy into a tent and then turned towards the pile of bodies. He kicked the bodies as if they were sacks of garbage and then urinated on them.

Seconds after the two left the main tent another man came out. He was a white man, looking about the same age as the leader of the attack. He was not dressed like the others. Instead he had a tropical print shirt like those Jack saw men wear at the resorts. He wore a squat dirty hat and was chewing on the stub of cigar. The man called the leader over to him in a tone Jack could tell was an order even if he couldn't understand the words. The cigar chewing man thumped his finger on the leader's chest and Jack could see the leader become weak the longer the man talked. When they finished the conversation, the white man walked to a jeep parked on the other side of the main tent.

As the man was climbing into the jeep he looked back in Jack's direction. Even though the length of a football separated them, Jack felt the man's eyes on him. A chill came over Jack as if he was hit with the first wave of a fever. Jack felt like this man was somehow going to be forever connected to his family. Even though Francis was safe in the States, he was suddenly terrified for him.

Before the man sat down in the jeep he threw his cigar into the pile of bodies. The mound went up in an instant roll of flame. A faint breeze blew down from the encampment and brought the smell of roasting meat. The man drove away into the darkness of the jungle. The leader, from Jack's vantage point yards away, seemed to be as shaken by the encounter.

Chapter 14

Monica was startled by the young boy falling into her tent. Immediately he started speaking to her in English. Calling her by the name she was known in the village, "Ms. M you must get out of here. They are going to kill you. The man who captured you thought you and your husband were American drug agents. He wanted you for the big reward offered for your capture. It would have made him a big man with the drug people. He found out now that you are only a school teacher. When his men learn of his mistake they will most likely turn on him and make fun of him and kill him and you. He wants me to convince you that you must act like you are an agent. It is the only way we can all stay alive. The other men did not hear what I heard on the radio. They still think you are a prize."

Chapter 15

Jack watched the jeep disappear into the jungle. He moved closer to the tents following the edge of the jungle grass. He could hear English spoken. He followed the sound to a tent across from the main tent. Two men stood guard outside, one in front and one in the back. Jack was sure that if Monica was anywhere, she was in that tent. Just as Jack made that discovery, the leader came back, stepped through the tent and pulled Monica out with him. Following behind was the boy. Two guards fell in line with them.

Jack took this opportunity to slip out of the brush and through the back flap of the tent. Inside he found the canteen of fresh water. He helped himself to a drink then replaced it as he found it. There was no place to hide except under the cot. He hoped they would bring Monica back and throw her in without looking. He pulled the gun from his waist and kept it tight against his chest.

The sun was starting to steal the darkness when the front flap opened and Monica fell into the tent. She fell with her back to Jack still hiding under the cot. Jack reached around her back without touching her so that she could see his hand with his wedding band. He didn't want her to jump or scream.

Monica rolled over on the ground to stare into Jack's eyes. Jack lifted the gun to his lips gesturing her silence. Monica moved herself up to the cot the best she could with two limp arms. Jack worked to get to his feet, knowing that he had to make something happen now or they would be lost forever.

Without warning the flap of the tent flipped back. Standing silhouetted by the rising sun was the leader. Jack fell back at the surprise and found himself looking up at the man that two days ago changed their lives. Jack brought the gun up level with the man and pulled the trigger. The sound rang his ears and the whole tent filled with the acrid smell of gun smoke. The man stumbled back releasing his grip on the center pole of the tent as his hand went to the shoulder hit by the bullet. With his free hand, he pulled a bush knife from his belt and charged towards Jack. Jack pointed the gun again at the man now only inches away from the barrel. Jack hesitated one second to long. The blade from the leader's knife found its mark in Jack's chest, severing crucial arteries.

Jack turned to see Monica trying to get off the cot to push the man out of the way. That was the last thing Jack saw as he fell back with his knees bent under him. The man finished him by kicking him over on his side. Then he turned and punched Monica across the face sending her back down on the cot.

The young boy was standing outside the tent and saw all that happened. He wanted to reach for Monica but was frozen in fear. He knew if he went against this powerful man, he would be next. The other men, hearing the shot, were now outside the tent. The leader ordered them to drag Jack's body out of the tent and throw him on the burning pile with the others. He then ordered the two original guards to bring Monica back to the main tent.

Chapter 16

Monica couldn't erase the image of the knife sinking into Jack's chest. Her eyes were searching all around the tent looking for something to distract the image from her mind. Laying on a crate by the radio under a gun the leader had been carrying was their letter. Francis would never see the letter or learn why they loved the people of this village. All he would know in the future was maybe how they died.

Lost in these thoughts Monica did not see the young boy walk into the tent. The boy walked up behind Monica and started to plead with her.

"Ms. M, I am so sorry. I could not stop these men. They forced me to come or else they would kill my family."

Monica, even in her condition had nothing but compassion for the boy. He was maybe just a year older than their son. She could only imagine what he had seen in his short years. Monica, asked the boy to retrieve the letter from the crate. He refused. To do so would have meant death. Monica pleaded again with him to bring it to her. As part of the bargain, Monica asked him to remove the wooden cross around her neck. The boy reached out, lifted the cross from her neck and shoved it in his pocket. As the boy was about to give in to Monica, the leader charged through the door.

Still in his angered state, his shoulder bloodied from the graze of the bullet, he walked over to the table and picked up the gun that had been holding down the letter. The letter dropped to the muddy floor of the tent. The leader stepped out of the tent. Seconds later the boy and Monica heard repeated gun shots. One of the men fell back into the tent, bleeding from a shot in his chest.

The boy pulled Monica from the chair by her shirt and raced towards the radio. He grabbed the letter laying on the ground, shoved it into a tattered pocket of his shorts and continued pushing Monica through the back of the tent. Looking back, Monica and the boy saw the man systematically picking off the men remaining in the camp.

Monica stopped too long.

Seeing his prize fleeing, the leader turned the gun in Monica's direction. One shot was all it took to drop her to her to the ground. The boy, now deep in the cover of the jungle, knew it was better to keep running. He reached in and felt the letter stuck in his pocket. He knew he had to get rid of the letter, but he couldn't just throw it away.

When he made it back to village a day later his first stop was the priest's hut. He stuck the letter in the priest's door where villagers often left notes for him. He knew the priest would know what to do with the letter. Then he left the village knowing he could never contact his family again.

The Philadelphia Dispatch July 25, 1980
Two missionary workers were found murdered in Brazil. Their badly decomposed bodies were discovered along with other bodies yet to be identified. Jack and Monica Stratton, both natives of the North Philadelphia area. The couple were in their last year working with the Peace Corps. They leave behind their son Francis Stratton currently a sixth-grade student at Our Lady of Hope grade school.

Part Two

What Goes Around, Comes Around

Chapter 1

U.S. Marine Camp, Amazon Jungle 1999

Captain Francis Stratton wiped sweat from his face. The towel he grabbed was already wet from the jungle humidity. Sweat continued to drip from a one day's growth of stubble on his chin. He slid his fingers through the high and tight cut that left enough of the oily black hair on top to confirm at thirty he was in no danger of losing his hair anytime soon.

A single light bulb hanging from the ceiling flickered with the inconsistent power of the camp generator. He threw the towel in the corner of a hut he called home and peeled the olive drab T-shirt now almost black with perspiration over his head.

His naked torso revealed how seriously he took his workouts. A tattoo of a snake curling down a tree trunk wrapped around a well-developed bicep covered his right arm. A simple cross with a crown of thorns hanging in the cross beam covered his left.

Francis loved night runs through the jungle and village. The patrols cleared paths through the jungle to make it easier to move around especially at night. Francis enjoyed utilizing these paths, many of them running close to the Amazon River. The trails reminded him of running along the Schuylkill River back in Philly. Captain Stratton, a Jesuit priest and chaplain for the unit, saw little need for letting down his workout routine because he was in the middle of a jungle.

Stratton's legs were further testimony to his running habit. The upper thighs stretching out of the issued running shorts were tanned and hard. Right now, the shorts were sticking to him from the sweat giving them more the look of wet swimming trunks rather than runners shorts.

The Marine detachment was assigned to help the local people fight and protect their villages from the drug lords who were victimizing and enslaving the people. Captain Francis volunteered for this assignment. In doing so he gave up the opportunity to stay behind and work in the safer environment of parish or academic life. Ever since the death of his parents in these jungles he wanted to understand what they went through working with the people in these villages and what drove them to stay amid the dangers that were always present.

No enlisted man or officer in the detail ever doubted Francis' commitment as a Marine. The men saw him as a hard ass Marine first, priest second. Francis knew that was their opinion of him, but he knew himself, he was more priest than Marine. He hoped he would never be tested to prove otherwise.

Francis was one of those guys that had no clue of how good he looked. It never concerned him. Growing up with his grandparents he followed their habit of keeping everything plain. It was not their practice to draw attention. Keep your mind clean and your body strong were the two-main preaching's of his grandmother. Once ordained, he followed a common Jesuit tradition of rarely dressing in clerical attire. When he was in the States, this caused more than a few problems when women would start flirting with him having no idea he was a priest. He wasn't quick to pick up on their clues. His grandmother often told him his looks were going to be his biggest problem as a priest.

Even in the jungle he didn't wear the uniform in the manner he should. He felt he didn't deserve the uniform in the same way the men who were risking their lives. It wasn't unusual for a recruit to mistake Captain Francis as a civilian rather than a Marine officer. He became a Marine Chaplain because he wanted to work with those who put their life on the line. He wanted them to know that someone was there for them no matter what, but he doubted he could ever do what they did. Francis was trained to preserve life, they were trained to take it if necessary.

Francis was still dripping from the run and jungle humidity and trying his best to dry off when a woman carrying her baby charged through the poor excuse for a door.

Chapter 2

The woman wasn't just any woman who burst through the door. Her name was Galina, the prize of the village and wife of Christian, one of the men who seemed to be well connected with one of the leading drug lords. She was also the mother of two children.

No one could argue against the fact Galina was the most beautiful of the village women. She was twenty years old and for some reason, spared the ravages of the hard life in the rainforest. Her smile set off pearl teeth next to bronze skin. To Francis, she looked more like the women seen in Sao Paulo. They were women who still carried some of the traits of their rainforest DNA but refused to admit it while living more like Fifth Avenue models.

Galina had a sense of style that was not usually found in these little isolated villages. Missionaries, much like Francis parents, must have taken the time to show her pictures of girls in magazines. Galina could put together clothes donated from support agencies that found their way to the village in a way that seemed odd in this wet green world. This made her stand out over and above her beauty and more than one Marine was warned to keep his hands off.

She was the only woman in the village that wore jeans and tonight she wore a pair that showed every curve and a white T-shirt that sported the logo of the Yankees. The white shirt set off the black hair that hung almost to her waist and partially covered the baby in her arms. Galina was not only stunning in her beauty she was also a strong woman, able to do the work many of the men could no longer handle. The young men of the village were pressed into service by the ruling drug lord, Hector Fuentes, who had a special attraction to this village and Galina. This left the old men to support the village while the young men were used as drug runners and hired guns in Hector's own private army.

Galina's husband, Christian, was one of Fuentes favorite workers. He was older than Galina and had a history with Fuentes that often made him cower under his orders. These demands took Christian away from his family, often overnight. This meant Galina their son and newborn daughter were alone in the village. For a woman like Galina to be alone with a man like Hector roaming the village was not good.

Christian always seemed eager to take care of Francis. He and Francis were close in age and Christian's command of English was better than most, so he made a good companion when Francis was in the village. He also helped to break the ice between Francis and some of the villagers who were suspicious of his intentions. Christian was also the only one in the village that could operate the two-way radio, the main communication with the outside world for the village. Christian operated the radio since he was a young boy and it was this skill that made him a valuable person to whoever needed information, especially Hector.

The radio was also the way Hector would send orders to Christian. The orders were coded in such a way that anyone listening would never understand what Hector really wanted. To the world listening in, it sounded like Christian was his foreman and all Hector was doing was lining up workers for the day. What he was really doing was gathering the next group of expendable carriers to move his drugs out of the jungle.

Chapter 3

It was obvious that Galina was upset. She would never burst into Francis' hut in such an abrupt manner without a good reason. Even as uncivilized as some wanted to make the villagers appear, they were always the models of respect and manners. They respected one another's privacy as much as they relied on each other's cooperation.

Galina placed the baby on a stack of pallets that made a makeshift table paying little attention to the almost naked priest in front of her. Most women outside the jungle would use this opportunity to take all of Francis' features in. For Galina it was more important to find a place to lay her baby Angelina down.

The baby carried her mother's beauty. In a few years there would be two remarkable and stunning women in this small patch of jungle. Angelina was the first baby he baptized when he came to the unit.

The advantage Galina had living with Christian was learning English. She could make herself understood with a little effort but right now, she rattled on excitedly in her native tongue which Francis still did not have a good grasp. Francis could only move around his hut trying to grab a shirt and pants all while trying to listen and calm Galina. Trying to use body language as well as words Francis looked like he was playing a pick-up game of charades.

"Galina, stop. I don't know what you are saying," trying to calm her with an outstretched hand which she batted it away as a futile gesture. She returned in English this time saying,

"Stop. Confess...I must confess to you."

Francis couldn't even imagine what this woman would need to confess with such urgency. Again, trying to calm her down he reached out, this time he didn't touch her. The baby began to cry which seemed to distract her anxiety.

"What is wrong Galina?"

"I must confess then God will help Christian."

Galina reached down on the table and pulled the baby Angelina close to her as if someone was going to snatch her from her arms. She knelt in front of Francis and made the best sign of the cross she could while holding the child. Looking down at her, Francis could understand as a man, why so many men were attracted to her. Her hair was so shinny it caught the reflection of the one light in the hut. Her chiseled cheekbones and watery brown eyes stirred an urge in Francis that he was not comfortable with. He wanted to reach out and cup her face in his hands but, he knew he couldn't. When he was ordained, he never really grasped what he was giving up.

Francis, knew it was useless to argue with Galina from this point. Whatever she needed, she needed it now. The early missionaries convinced the people that bad things came from sin and if they wanted good things to happen in their life they had to be without sin. This kept the confession box busy and justified the exploitation of the people by some of the former missionaries.

"Captain Father, I sinned with another man. Please forgive me."

In an uncharacteristic burst out of shock Francis said,

"Who?"

"Hector Fuentes. He comes to my home and sends Christian to the radio sometimes for days. When Christian is away he does things. He tells me he will kill Christian if I tell."

"Galina, this man is hurting you. Do you understand? You are not sinning."

"No Captain Father, God must forgive me so that I can pray to God to save Christian and my little boy and baby"

"Galina, God forgives you. Where is Christian now?"

"I don't know, he went away with Hector two days ago. I have not seen him and now Hector wants Angelina. He says the baby belongs to him. She is Christian's child. I know she is. Mothers know."

Francis reached down and helped Galina to her feet. He moved books occupying the only chair in his hut and directed Galina and the baby to the chair. Francis offered her a warm bottle of water in hopes that it would help to calm her. Instead, Galina took the bottle and poured some of the clean water, a commodity this deep in the jungle, on a towel next to her and started to pat the fresh water on Angelina's face.

Francis was never good around babies. He never had to be, they weren't part of his childhood and as a priest he figured his only encounter would be an occasional baptism. This baby was different. She pulled at Francis with her eyes as if she knew some secret. Francis, without thinking, reached over and took Angelina from Galina's arms. The child's skin was already the copper color of her mother's and her hair now over her ears, was deep and dark with streaks of blue as the light hit the side of her head. Francis cradled the baby in his arms and the two stared at each other as if they were trying to communicate but didn't know what to say. Still holding the child, Francis turned to Galina who was now sitting with both hands covering her face in a shame.

"Galina, where do you think Christian is? Where did Hector send him?"

"I don't know. Hector came to us two days ago and pulled Christian outside. He was beating on Christian and yelling about a letter. Hector grabbed our son who was trying to stop Hector. Hector picked up our son and then he told Christian he was taking Angelina also if he did not get the letter. He lied to Christian and told him Angelina was his baby. Christian, turned on Hector. He began yelling at Hector and at one point, raised his fist to Hector. Hector slapped Christian across his face then stomped on him when he was down. My son tried to hit Hector when Christian was down, but he slapped him also. Two of Hector's men dragged them both away. I have not seen Christian or our son since. God needs to save them Captain Father."

Chapter 4

Francis never expected to be a family counselor especially in the middle of the jungle. He figured the closest to family work would be if some Marine got one of the locals pregnant. This situation with Galina put him in the middle of a husband, drug lord, a mother and the little angel he was holding in his arms.

Francis walked over to Galina. It was hard for him not to reach out and hug her. He was surprised at how those emotions were working on him. The only woman he ever really hugged was his grandmother and he found the emotion now so foreign. What surprised him even more was that he didn't want to put the baby down. Francis touched Galina on the shoulder remembering how she reacted with the last touch.

"Galina go home. If Christian comes home, he will be looking for you. You need to be there when he returns. I'll ask the Marines to look for him. They know how to find Hector and his men."

Francis knew his promises were empty, but he had to say something. Galina stood up and stared at Francis. He knew she didn't believe a word of what he said. She was too smart for that. She reached for the baby and took her back in her arms. As they left the hut the baby continued to look back at Francis. Francis somehow knew those eyes would be with him for the rest of his life.

Francis decided that was enough counseling for the day. The benefits of the run were long gone. There was more tension in his body now than before the run. He pulled a warm beer from his stash in an old red and white cooler he brought from home. He moved to the stoop of his hut to listen to the jungle sounds as night settled in.

Chapter 5

The jungle sounds were absent tonight. A village dog barked. A few Marines gathered in a tent about ten yards away were singing a bad rendition of "Proud Mary." The jungle chorus he was hoping for was silent. Too quiet. Francis stayed on the stoop until the beer was gone. The beer did little to relieve his thirst or his frustration. He wished he could change the situation for Galina and her family, but right now he was powerless. In the morning he would speak to a few of the Marines to stay alert for Christian and his boy. Maybe once the Marines gathered the hard evidence they were looking for on Fuentes, all of this would be over and Galina and her family could be whole again.

Francis stepped inside the same time a helicopter flew so low over the encampment that the rotor wash blew the flimsy mosquito cloth hanging over the windows of the hut.

"The night patrol is back early," Francis said trying to break his own silence in the hut.

Immediately after the pass, the stinging odor of diesel fuel spilled in through the open windows. Francis turned to go back out the door when a blast blew him back and laid him out on the hut floor.

Chapter 6

Opening his eyes, he squinted from the light of the fire that surrounded him. Making his way to the door he could hear a chopper making a return pass. He watched from his hands and knees as the helicopter spilled more diesel over the village. Flares launched from outside the village arched over and down into the oily mess exploding in flashes of fire when they touched the fuel. Marines were running from tents, some dressed only in boxers and T-shirts. Screams began coming from the village as fire storms raced between huts.

The huts went up in seconds as some were nothing more than jungle grass, old shipping crate lumber and branches pulled together. Two more choppers came on the scene landing just beyond the fire perimeter. Men armed with automatic weapons poured out of the helicopters. As the villagers ran from the flames, they were picked off by the attackers with no mercy shown to women, children or old men. Bodies became obstacles as others tried to flee the flames and gunfire. The silence only seconds ago was replaced with the roar of fire, screams and automatic weapon fire.

The Marines moved into a position to defend their encampment but were cut off by fire from any good defensive positions. A second wave of men turned their assault on the Marines killing the soldiers with ease from the attacker's position of cover. Two Marines came running to Francis's position. Francis crawled outside hoping to stay below the smoke and not expose himself to the bullets flying everywhere. A figure was running directly at Francis. Flames trailing behind the person as they ran. There was someone else close behind. As they came closer it was Galina in front caring the baby. The baby was wrapped tight in blankets shielding her from the flames crawling up the back of Galina. Francis raised to his knees. The two Marines reached him at the same time. In rapid succession, both Marines were hit and fell at Francis's feet. When Galina came close, Francis could make out the figure of Fuentes behind her. Galina stumbled and the baby rolled towards Francis like a soccer ball passed on the field. Smoke rose around Galina's body as Hector stood over her, one leg on either side of her. Francis reached for the sidearm of the dead Marine beside him. Hector saw what Francis was doing. Francis pulled the gun from the Marine's side and raised it at Hector. Hector looked directly at Francis and then leveled one shot into Galina's head.

Francis watched her body bounce up then rest smoldering on the damp jungle floor. He dropped back in horror.

He wanted to pull the trigger but couldn't.

Chapter 7

Francis scrambled on his knees and retrieved the baby, crying and still wrapped tight. Francis scooped the baby and rolled back in enough time to see Fuentes charging at him with a knife. Hector kicked the gun away from Francis and with one swing of his arm sliced the knife across Francis stomach. Francis felt the heat of his own blood spilling over his side. Hector reached down and grabbed the bundle that was the child and threw it off to the side landing it in smoldering wood the remains of a makeshift chapel. Francis tried to get up and crawl to the child but a kick in the chin by Hector's boot knocked him unconscious. Fuentes stood over the helpless Francis.

"Priest you are as weak as your father."

Chapter 8

Francis was roused by one of the village dogs licking the back of his neck. He tried to roll over and face the sky. His head was pounding from the blow he took from Fuentes. He was finally able to sit up and look around. In front of him what was once thick green vegetation and proud huts of the villagers was now charred black. Bodies everywhere, some still smoldering. A few of them recognizable by Francis.

Francis looked over where he remembered Galina laying. Her body was burned beyond recognition. He only knew that was where she was supposed to be. The dog that licked his face was pawing at something laying half in a puddle of water. Francis crawled over as fast as the pain allowed. He swiped the dog away catching it across the snout. Wrapped in burnt blankets was Angelina. One side of her face burnt, the thick hair gone, her little arm was burnt to her shoulder. The half of her body that was laying in the water and protected by the wet blankets was as pure as it was hours ago. Francis pulled all the blankets from the child as the baby let out a scream of pain. Suddenly she stopped crying as if she was not going to surrender to the pain.

The baby Angelina and Francis laid spread out together surrounded by what was once their life. Francis, Angelina, and the dog, the only three forms of life left in the charred jungle. Francis wrapped the baby in what was left of the blankets and then tended to his own body. He slowly raised the shirt that was stuck to his chest with dried blood and mud. The mud sealed the cut for now but that didn't stop the bugs from crawling in and out of the slash. Francis felt a wave of panic and faint come over him. He looked over at the baby. Angelina returned his stare with eyes too hard for a baby.

Francis stood up. Turning full circle, he could see farther than ever before. What was once obstructed with thick jungle vegetation was now a blackened open field. Nothing was left. The fire had destroyed everything along with evidence of who attacked them. The only witnesses were Francis and the baby.

Then Francis heard them. Helicopters coming in from behind him. Francis felt relief knowing that they would be rescued. He turned to watch the two Marine attack helicopters land only yards from them. Debris flew away from the rotor wash like sawdust blown by a fan. Francis covered Angelina with his body as he watched the rotors slow to an idling speed. Once the dust settled Francis had a clear view of the aircrafts. The pilots in both aircrafts were staying with their machines. Out of the open side of the first chopper a man emerged dressed like the attackers from last night. Two more came out dressed the same and they immediately started scanning the ruins. Francis watched as one kicked a body to make sure the person was dead.

It was too late for Francis to hide. Where would he go? Francis lifted the baby from the ground and held on to her careful not to press on her wounds. Francis watched as a person stepped from the second chopper. This person was not dressed like the other militia. Once out of the shadow of the chopper, Francis could tell it was Christian. Christian walked directly over to Francis and Angelina. Christian had the look of a man who just endured mental torture, his body was intact but there was no soul left. He had camouflaged backpack slung over his right shoulder.

Francis gently transferred the baby to her father's arms being careful of her burns.

"Christian, what's going on? Where have you been? Your wife is dead. Your baby is not far from death."

Tears streamed down Christians face, leaving streaks in the dirt on his face. Christian only responded,

"I am sorry. I have no choice. He is still holding my son. I could not save your parents or my wife, but I can save you and my children."

"What do you mean, what does any of this have to do with my parents?"

Christian reached in to his shirt with his free hand and grabbed a leather cord that was around his neck. He pulled the cord out the entire length letting a wooden cross suspended at the end, hang in front of him. Francis made a desperate attempt to reach for the cross, but he only swung at air. Christian turned his back on Francis and walked back to the idling choppers.

Chapter 9

Christian went to the farthest chopper and talked to the two men standing guard. He said something to them at the same time they looked back at Francis and laughed then they boarded the helicopter. What they didn't see was Christian pulling something out of the backpack and attaching it to the side of the chopper. Christian strolled casually back to the chopper that landed him. The chopper with the two men lifted off while Christian's chopper stayed on the ground. Once the chopper climbed to what would have been the tree line it exploded in a fireball. Francis felt the heat blow back to earth as it crashed into the charred village.

When Francis looked to the remaining helicopter he watched Christian move forward through the open door of the craft. The crack of a small caliber came from inside as the pilot slumped forward. Christian pulled the pilot and slid him out the open hatch. Francis could see the silhouette of man, the obvious profile of Hector moving forward and taking the pilot's position. Francis and the dog watched the helicopter until it was a dot in the sky.

Chapter 10

One Day Later

Francis rolled over on his side and was jolted awake by the smell of clean sheets. A navy nurse was wiping his head as he slowly regained awareness of where he was.

"Hello Father. It is good to have you back. Glad you could rest. I'll be right back."

Francis watched as she stepped out the door. When the door swung open Francis could see two MP's stationed outside the door. The nurse returned with a Marine doctor with major rank on his lapels. He was followed by a plainclothes man dressed like a tourist. The doctor addressed Francis as an officer.

"Captain, how do you feel? You gave us a scare. You're a lucky man. The slice in your side was infected deep into your stomach. I am afraid only God pulled you through this one.

"Captain," looking back at the tourist dressed visitor, "this man needs to speak to you. But only if you feel up to it. He has five minutes no more." The major turned to the nurse and gave the order.

"Five minutes and absolutely no more."

The man approached the side of Francis bed. He introduced himself as Balifour. He smelled of sweat, stale cigar and sulfur like someone just struck a match. The odor immediately made Francis dislike him. The man leaned into Francis as if he was a long-lost family member and was going to give him a kiss as a family greeting.

Francis was disliking him with each breath. Francis looked at the clock on the wall at the end of the bed. Only four more minutes with this man. Francis didn't feel like himself. Normally he would be very tolerant of someone like this. He felt like there was a stranger living in his body controlling his attitude.

"Captain, it is so nice to meet you in person. I had the pleasure of knowing your parents."

The way he said parents made Francis feel shivers through his body.

"Your mother was such a pretty little thing. So unfortunate what they did to her. Your father on the other hand. He was a lot like you. No guts. No action. How does it feel Captain to know you are the one that made my job easy?"

Francis getting more agitated looked at the clock. Three more minutes.

"You need to leave mister. I don't know who or what you are trying to pull."

"You know me. You've been battling me for a long time and you didn't even know it did you? You rest, I'll be back to check on you. You have a nice day Captain Father."

Francis hollered for the nurse,

"Nurse get this man out of here."

"Sir, there is no one in here. The Major is out in the hall with the guard and he and I are the only two that have been in here."

The smell from Balifour's presence lingered in the room.

"Can't you smell that stench nurse? He was just here? You were here when the Major brought him in. You were here…"

"You relax sir, I'll get the Major and we will get something to help you sleep. Francis realized who just visited him. He leaned over the bed rails and vomited all over the floor.

Chapter 11

The Next Day Balifour walked into the room, this time unannounced. Francis was half asleep still feeling the effects of the pain killers mixed with sleeping aids. He was not really able to sleep. The images of the last days continued to play in his head. His feeling of being disconnected from himself plagued him. He tried to pray more than once but couldn't even muster the words. It was as if he had a fight with God. He thought this must be what it is like when a spouse gives the other the silent treatment.

"If God wants to talk, he has some apologizing to do first."

It was Balifour's odor that fully awakened Francis.

"Good morning Father. Happy to see you are awake. You look better today than yesterday."

Balifour leaned back over Francis while at the same time unfolding a crumpled 5X7 photo.

"I think you know this man?"

In the picture was Christian. His hands displayed gunshot wounds in the palms. His feet were bound and it looked like one shot went through both feet. There was a blood stain in the center of the chest and his once perfect hairline was now a jagged cut that went across his forehead. Absent from around his neck was the leather cord and cross. Above Christian's head was a sign scribbled on pages ripped from a book. When Francis looked deeper he realized they were pages from a Bible. *"I will always win. Your God will always loose."*

Balifour ripped the photo up, walked into the connecting bathroom and flushed it down the commode. Francis tried to rise out of bed but the cut across his stomach forced him back down. Balifour walked out of the room. His odor clung to Francis' sheets and pillow. Francis frantically hit the nurses call button. He kept hitting it as if the more times he pressed it the faster help would come. By the time a nurse responded, Francis' bed linens were soaked with sweat and he was mumbling in a delirious state about a visit from the devil and a baby. None of the nurses could recall anyone but the Major and other nurses visiting or tending to Francis.

Part Three

Necessary Sin

Chapter 1

Sunday Night, Present Day

Tonight's patrol was miserable. The day long rain did nothing towards cooling down the air. The air-conditioner in the jeep was constantly fogging up the windshield because of the humid night air. Lightning lit up the convenience store as Sheriff August Hawk splashed his jeep through two massive potholes at the entrance of the local "Fill and Go" gas station. The slow roll of thunder like a bowling ball down a hollow lane followed him into the store. He was after the fourth cup of coffee of the night. The jeep was still running keeping the cab cool. A couple of the locals were hanging around the coffee machine as if it was a slot machine about to start spitting out quarters. Bill Colestock, owner of the diner on Main Street, was just finishing a call on his cell,

"Okay, I did my part. I made the call. I just hope you come through for me," snapping the aging flip phone closed. Surprising Bill from behind August said,

"That sounds serious Bill, you okay?"

Red faced, Bill turned to August trying to hide his surprise,

"Good evening Sheriff, rough night out there isn't it?"

August gave Bill a nod yes and a one finger hello to the other guys while he held a cup under the coffee spout. The guys new better than to try and engage August in conversation when he was working. August was too serious for most of them anyway. They respected him and knew if they needed him he would always be on his game.

Running out from the convenience store, ducking like people do in rain as if that keeps them dry, Sheriff Hawk slopped most of the coffee out of the cup. He slammed the jeep door disgusted over the rain, dropped the coffee in the cup holder and wiped the sloshed coffee off his hands on to his jeans. He tossed his rain-soaked ball cap across the seat and ran his right hand back over his head. His fingers dug furrows through his hair separating his graying hair into four shallow wet rows. He kept his hair cropped short on the sides but still liked to have a little on top to prove he was not losing it like others his age. The two potholes splashed more coffee out as he pulled back on the highway. A flash of lightning killed the street light outside the Fill-N-Go. Thunder vibrated the loose jeep doors.

Bill Colestock checked his watch and gave August a couple of minutes head start. He was nervous now, he came so close to blowing the whole thing. He did his part but now curiosity was getting the best of him.

The dispatch radio in the jeep was turned off. August hated driving around with that thing squawking back at him. Most of the time it was someone complaining about a barking dog, loud music or some spouse coming home drunk. He turned the radio back on and immediately started picking up chatter from the accident site. The accident call came in while he was getting his coffee. The oily faced teenage clerk at the "Fill-N-Go" had to call him to the phone to connect him with the fire chief at the scene. August knew instinctively what to expect when he arrived at these scenes.

Chapter 2

August preferred his jeep over the county provided patrol car. The old jeep was a gift from a friend years ago. It was starting to show some wear just like August. The rain was dripping through the back of the canvas top. The paint job was hard to identify. It was probably red at one time. Tonight, it was brown and rust. There was an extra cake of mud on the fenders from plowing through a corn field earlier in the day. There were no lights on the jeep to identify it as a sheriff vehicle, but he did have a siren installed, which, in two years since elected sheriff, he had only used once. He often joked that he and the jeep would probably retire together. When the jeep stopped, that's when he was going to stop.

August was thinking to himself,

"These late night waterlogged wrecks never have a good ending. The rain makes everything worse for everyone."

The jeep's wipers stuttered across smeared grasshoppers and other assorted bugs that came to an end on his windshield during his afternoon's patrol. Between the rain, bug streaks and oncoming traffic it wasn't an easy night to drive even for someone who spends most of their time on the road. August took a sip from the coffee as he waited for the light to change to make the left turn east on to HW160. A car passed on his left with an expired inspection sticker. It wasn't worth it tonight. Another sip of coffee and he was calming down a little. Lightning flashed followed immediately by thunder. The rain sounded like a bathroom shower on the canvas roof of the jeep. Another sip of coffee.

"Nothing tastes better than coffee on a night like this," he said out loud like someone was sitting beside him. He did that a lot.

Highway 160 a Nebraska highway that is busy with farm equipment, cars and grain trucks between Watercreek and Dunbar during the day. At night, you could walk down the middle of it and not be in too much danger. For an accident to happen out here now was not good. August figured, it was probably some drunk or a teenager that just got their license and was showing off. August was hoping it wasn't going to be the latter. Like any cop, the worse part of the job was informing the next of kin especially if it was a young person.

As August pulled up to the accident scene, one of the volunteer firemen was standing in the middle of the road working traffic control. August's lights hit the reflective strips on the volunteer's turnout gear making the fireman look like a dancing neon robot waving a flare. The whole scene reflected as a mirror image back on the wet road. Red, amber and blue lights along with the white spotlights directed at the scene, gave a serious scene a carnival atmosphere.

August pulled off to the side and could see the point where the car went off the road. Deep ruts were cut into the field showing a clear path to the accident. A sign giving direction to highway 75 and 160 was flattened and pointing in the opposite direction. The guardrail was peeled back like a ribbon. Slicks of black paint stretched along the rail. The rain, steaming off the road, mixed with the fragrance from the blossoming corn in the field adjacent to the road added its own earthy smell. It wasn't a bad smell until it joined with the diesel exhaust from the trucks. Fog swirled around the feet of the first responders and hid the tires of the fire trucks making them look suspended. Lightning snapped.

Stepping from the jeep August pulled a mud stained yellow slicker from a hook behind his seat and reached over to take one more sip of now cold coffee. Slicking one hand over his hair and with the other he pulled a well-worn John Deere ball cap down to eyebrow level. Walking on to the scene, he looked like a farmer from the area just stopping by out of curiosity.

August walked along the road, snapping the slicker together, he was calculating in his head how this might have happened. Shouts from the first responders were numb to him as he focused on the tracks through the mud leading to a black SUV hanging on the edge of a drainage ditch. He could hear the water running off from the field passing under the vehicle. From where he stood he could tell the vehicle rolled at least once. There was a body lying on the other side of the road covered in protective yellow tarps.

"God, I hope it is not some kid."

Driver or passenger it was too early to tell. Closer to the scene, he could smell the ugly odor of burnt rubber and vehicle fluids. Stan Farley, owner of the hardware store in Watercreek and a Lieutenant with the Watercreek rural fire department stopped August from getting any closer.

"August, you need to know something about this wreck."

"What's wrong Stan?"

"I hate to tell you this August, its Fr. Steve's SUV. He also had a passenger with him. Some young woman. We found her about ten feet outside of the vehicle. It appears she was thrown through the window. We don't know who she is. We might know better once we can get in the vehicle. Father Steve is still alive; we need to use the jaws to get him out. He's hurt, Sheriff. I've never seen a car banged up this bad and someone survive. He's asking for you August."

The weight of the news about Fr. Steve pushed August down on the guard rail next to the idling fire pumper. The rain was suddenly cold for July. Rain hitting the brim of his ball cap sounded like pebbles smacking cardboard. He watched as drops rolled around the brim and then drop off like lemmings jumping off a cliff one after another. The drone of the diesel matched his heartbeat. All the memories of Steve, his introductions and support were overwhelming him. The one person that could call him by his right name might be gone. A car passed behind him and August felt the spray blow back against him. Lightning blued the scene. August knew who the woman was laying under the tarp on the asphalt.

Chapter 3

It seemed his whole world was centered on that guardrail. If he stayed there, none of this would be real. If he moved life would leap back into action. August finally forced himself off the rail and deeper into the scene. August never even realized Stan was still standing next to him just waiting for him to move. August flicked on his small tactical light and cast it a few steps ahead. Some of the firemen were standing around with their hands in the pockets of their turnout gear as casual as if they were discussing last night's Royal's baseball score. August knew what their topic of discussion really was. More than once, one of them turned back towards the tarp covered mound on the opposite side of the road. August gave them a look that turned their conversation to immediate embarrassment.

When August reached the black Ford SUV it was perched at an angle looking as if it would roll again any minute. The roof was caved close to the top of the front seats. The windows were all blown out and the front windshield folded back into the driver's compartment. Much of the hood followed behind the windshield. Deflated air bags hung limp and white powder from them coated the inside.

The emergency lights stuttered the movement of everyone in the scene creating a grisly horror movie. Through the passenger window August could see Fr. Steve slumped over the wheel, his head bent to the side by the roof pushing down. The white hair that in any other situation made him appear like a distinguished captain of a cruise ship, was now wet from the rain, matted and red with blood. Rain hitting his face washed blood down the side and ponded on his shoulder. Stan ordered two young firemen down to help August move around the slippery embankment.

Moving to the driver's side against the advice of the firemen, August made his way to the front door. The two responders put their weight to the SUV, fearful of it moving.

"Steve!" "Steve!" August felt the rain running down his back under the slicker as he leaned in to Steve. Hollering again. No response.

Reaching through the window, August grabbed Steve's hand which still had a solid grip on the wheel. Steve moved at the touch.

"Steve, its August."

Unable to move his head to August, Steve moved his eyes as far to the left as he could.

"August, this is not good. I think my neck is broken. I can't feel my legs, I am not sure they are even there. I can feel something in my side. I can't tell you what happened. I must have blacked out. Where is she?" Steve began to get very agitated.

"She is out of the car Steve. Don't worry, we need to get you out of here."

"I am not getting out Auggie. You know that... I have things I need to tell you."

August knew Steve was slipping away fast. August tightened the grip on his friend's hand. He could feel the cold limb that was being fed by death rather than blood. August knew that feeling all too well. August worked at holding back tears. He could feel his gut getting tighter in response to his tension. The rain suddenly picked up intensity. Bouncing off the metal it made it harder to hear Steve.

"You know what I am going to ask you and you need to do it for me. We have to do it now."

The two of them had joked many times about this possible scenario and like two teenage blood brothers they made each other a promise. August never took it serious but now what was said in jest was coming back to haunt him. Steve stammered the words August did not want to hear,

"You... need.... to hear my confession."

Chapter 4

The responders holding August and the car heard the request. The two responders looked at each other with the expression of,

"What do we do now?"

August backed away from the vehicle. What he was asking was impossible.

"Steve, I can't do that I am not a priest anymore."

Steve could only muster a slight turn of his eyes in the direction of August. Blood was sliding down Steve's chin from the corner of this mouth.

"Augie, we don't have time to argue. You made a promise, don't let my soul down now. You will find out things later, I know you. I need forgiveness now. You know you can do it. You don't have a choice."

August ordered the two responders to the far ends of the vehicle. He leaned in as close as he dared without adding weight to the SUV. Steve, started,

"God forgive me of my failings. I have betrayed many that are close. Forgive me."

August sensed that Steve was talking more to him than God.

"August, take care of our people..." Steve didn't finish.

August's only friend was gone. August whispered in Steve's ear hoping there was just one breath of life left,

"Go in peace my friend, God forgives you. I forgive you."

With his thumb extended, August reached in and traced the sign of the cross on Steve's bloody scalp. When he finished he let his thumb linger on Steve's forehead shocking himself how instinctively he carried out the act.

He was thrown back thirty years when a desperate woman, Galina, was kneeling in front of him begging for God's forgiveness. Just like Steve minutes after he administered the sacrament, she was dead and August life changed forever. If only he had pulled the trigger then, maybe they would both be alive today.

Chapter 5

A new smell coming from the interior of the car caught August. The smell of day old cigar stench mixed with remnants of a fresh struck match. The recognition of the smell almost knocked August off his feet.

The two responders, who obviously heard enough, looked at August like they had never seen him before and he didn't belong at this scene. The sheriff they knew was just addressed like a priest. August glared at them with his best Marine stone face. He knew what they were thinking. He accepted their help back to the road.

He suddenly felt old and tired.

When he reached the highway deck, the sound of the jaws crunching metal echoed off the idling trucks. A sickening sound. He thought how lucky relatives of victims are never hearing that sound. A pop startled August followed by the stretching groan of metal as the firemen bent the roof back. Lightning danced through the western sky displaying towering thunderheads connected by spiderwebs of light. Thunder was seconds coming. August walked over to the yellow tarp. Puddles formed in the valleys of the tarp mimicking the body underneath. Bending down on one knee, August pulled back the canvas. It wasn't the woman he expected to find.

Chapter 6

Even with the bruises and twisted disfigurement to the body from the wreck, August knew he was not looking at the woman Steve was bringing him to meet tomorrow. Her body was contorted like the dead roadside deer he passed on his daily drives. Steve was taking with him secrets bigger than just August's history.

Standing up and looking back at the responders August could read their lips and he knew what happened down below raced through the radios and whispers like a bunch of cackling women sitting around Trish's Beauty Shop on a Saturday morning.

August walked back to the jeep then turned back for one more look at the scene. The lights were distorted by the rain. He let his mind wonder and it trailed back many years. He saw the beautiful Galina kneeling in front of him holding her baby begging for God's forgiveness for her sins. Her beauty such a relief from the tortured faces and bodies on many of the villagers he dealt with daily. Again, he fought back the tears and the pit growing in his stomach. He turned the jeep around in the middle of the highway and drove back to town. He stopped before he hit the city limits to throw up and let the tears flow.

While the door was still open the pain hit. August doubled over against the steering wheel. His left arm felt like it took a punch from a ghost attacker. His chest tightened, and he pulled his right arm in. He rolled to the left and fell out on to the road, his face making the first contact with the pavement. The John Deere cap rolled to the center of the highway.

Chapter 7

Bill Colestock spotted August's idling jeep. He was a surprised to see him face down on the road. That wasn't part of the plan, but he thought to himself it might get him what he wants quicker than they promised. He walked across the highway hoping to find August dead. As he got closer August called his name.

"Jesus Auggie, what the hell happened to you?"

"Bill, thank God it's you. Get me up. I'll be okay just help me up."

"You look pretty bad Auggie, let me take you to the hospital."

"No, just get me up in the jeep. I think my arm might be broke."

Helping August up in the jeep,

"You are one stubborn Marine."

Bill walked to the middle of the highway and picked up the ball cap. He came back to the jeep handed the cap to August.

"It was Fr. Steve, Bill. He didn't make it."

"I am sorry to hear that Auggie, he was a good man. I know the two of you were good buddies. Not much of a church guy myself you know, but I always liked him. You sure you don't want me to at least follow you to the hospital? That arm and your face looks pretty messed up. You almost ruined that precious tattoo of yours."

"I am fine, I'll see a doctor tomorrow."

Bill climbed back in his truck and thought to himself,

"SOB, I should have let him lay there. This better pay off like they promised."

Chapter 8

August struggled driving back to Watercreek with one good arm and straining to see out of a wet windshield with one eye. He instinctively pulled in the parking lot of St. Mary. Once there, he had no real recollection of pulling in.

He sat and stared at the blurry image of the church. The light from a few security lights inside the church backlit the elaborate stained-glass windows. He was sitting in front of the window of Jesus in the Garden of Olives. The scene depicted Jesus bent over a rock begging God to take away the pain that was about to come. The image held August for more than an hour. The only sound was his own breath passing in and out and rain tapping on the jeep roof.

Fixed on the window, August broke his own silence by speaking out loud.

"I can't even imagine what you were thinking. I've lived my life the best I know. You keep throwing me in situations that force me to doubt you. How can I return to a life you called me too when all I want to do is curse at you? You've taken everything away from me and given me nothing back. You've taken my parents, my vocation, and now my only friend.

I hate you as much as those who threw me into this situation. If I were Jesus at the garden, my response to you would not have been so compliant. Leave me alone and let me fix my own messes."

August ignored the pressure from his soul to go inside the church and continue his rant. A squawk on the radio broke in calling for a tow truck out at the accident scene. August reached over to the radio and almost broke the knob turning it off. He went through a lot of knobs.

No one in town would know about the accident yet but by morning the whole town would know. Internet and social networking had nothing on small town connections. August sat in the lot for a couple more minutes then decided to move on before someone spotted his jeep. No sense adding to the stories.

By the time August pulled into the driveway at home the rain stopped. Crickets were chirping as he walked up from the driveway. Mugginess in the air from the daytime heat wasn't cooled by the rain; it only served to remind him of a tropical night. A night thirty years ago that he thought was behind him until tonight. The swelling memories along with the loss of his friend brought him to his knees in the middle of the yard. August fell forward with no concern how he was going to land. He landed on the injured arm and he screamed in pain. He rolled on his back. The rain started again. It beat on his face, but he was glued to the ground as if hands were holding him down.

The rain sounded like helicopter chops making another pass over the village dropping its oily mixture covering everything it touched with its slick and deadly film. Fire balls launched from the village jungle borders. Within seconds the whole village was on fire. Villagers were running everywhere. A clap of thunder mirrored the shot from Hectors gun to the back of Galina's head. August saw her body rise and drop with the shot.

August was brought back by another clap of thunder. He struggled to get up with one arm. Drenched with mud and grass sticking to him he finally made it to his back door. The screen door slammed behind him as he walked through the unlocked door. August sat down on the closest kitchen chair and laid his head on the table and tried to pray this time rather than yell at God. The first prayers uttered in years. He felt like a child all alone, deep in hostile woods like those stories of lost kids in the fairy tales. He was surprised he could even form the words of a prayer.

"God, why are you tormenting me like this. Leave me alone, just let me go. I am not worthy of your time. I have lost everything you have given me, my parents, my grandparents, my friends, even my identity. I am a coward and a fraud. Just let me sleep and leave me alone."

Chapter 9

Monday

August woke from his spot at the table as the sun splashed through the window. His clothes were dry, but the mud and grass was still stuck on his face, arms and legs. His face ached from the fall and his eye was still partially swollen. Stretching his arm was painful, but at least it wasn't broken. He had patrol runs this morning and he couldn't do it in this condition. Coffee and a shower was all he wanted. His usual morning appetite was gone. He also knew the life he built so carefully in Watercreek was now over. By the end of the day, everyone would know some part of his past and what they didn't know they would make up.

August finished his shower and walked naked across the room to his closet. Fresh jeans and a polo shirt was his uniform of the day. Since the day he took office he vowed not to wear an official uniform. He had spent too many years dressed as something he wasn't. He believed the people who elected him knew him well enough. The casual dress gave him the appearance of being younger than he was. His body still reflected a strict and disciplined life, the two qualities that attracted him to the Jesuits and then the Marines. His grandparents were always after him to loosen up and relax but August always felt like he had some internal standard he had to meet. The women of the county loved how their sheriff looked. The men respected it.

Pulling the polo over his head stretched the scar that ran across his midsection cutting in half a respectable six pack. The action made him wince as he pulled the injured arm through the sleeves. He bent the arm slowly convinced he could work with it, but it wouldn't be of much use to him for the rest of the day. August grabbed his badge and stuck it in his back pocket and walked to the kitchen lured in by the smell of brewing coffee.

Chapter 10

Sitting in the chair where August spent most of the night was a woman dressed as casual as he was. Tight jeans that showed some wear as well as a figure that made other women jealous, a wrinkled white blouse which she purposely didn't button very far up and sandals exposing painted red toenails. Her smoky blonde hair was styled in a casual cut and fell just over her ears and dropped a small wisp of bangs down her forehead. If it was any other woman, August would have given her a second look and more respect.

The first words August spoke out loud since last night carried the scratchy tone of one who had a restless sleep.

"What the hell are you doing here?"

She straightened herself in the chair and said,

"That's no way to greet a lady who just made you coffee."

Running his fingers over his stomach like he was looking for something, August responded,

"The difference Madam Mayor, is that most ladies are welcome in my house. Again, why are you here?"

"August, I am not here to fight with you. I know you had a rough night. Besides August, you look like you need more than coffee this morning. You're a mess. What happened? You look like you were in an accident, not Fr. Steve. What can I do?"

The mayor stood up, more to try and diffuse his dislike for her by showing her figure rather than displaying any kind of sympathy,

"I am sorry for your loss. I know you and Fr. Steve were close."

August muttered a thank you while he poured coffee over the sink into a stained mug with a picture of the Arch in St. Louis. As she walked closer to August, now with her arms crossed in front of her as she eyed the serpent and tree tattoo as if it was the first time she saw it, pausing for just a second,

"But there is a bigger concern here. You apparently have not been completely honest with the people of this county and more importantly with me."

Taking his first sip of coffee, using it to delay the reaction building inside of him and speaking into his coffee mug,

"So, what's your point?"

"My point? My God Sheriff, you are not what you sold to us as voters!"

"Do you feel like I sold myself to the people? If you remember, I was practically railroaded into the position. Did you vote for me Susan?"

"I did."

"Have I done a good job?"

"From what I can tell, yes."

August bowed slightly as if he was in the presence of royalty,

"Then Madam Mayor, with all due respect, get out of my house. You might think you are, but you are not my boss. I work for the people of this county. I have a job to do and the voters wouldn't appreciate you delaying my work day."

August walked over to the door, kicked the screen door open and with a foot stuck on the threshold against the screen and held it open until Susan walked out. August's callousness had the effect he hoped. Susan slammed the door of her car and pulled away with obvious attitude, her tires spitting sand off the asphalt road.

Susan Park is the second term mayor of Watercreek. Most people found Susan attractive. She made a good appearance for the city and the people were proud to have her as mayor, but they also knew not to ruffle her feathers. Something August usually ignored. The ironic thing, many lunch counter and beauty shop discussions, carried out by the local gossips, agreed on what a great couple the two of them would make.

After watching Susan drive up the road towards the Courthouse, August stepped back into the kitchen and slumped into his chair at the table. He hoped the shower and last night's sleep would erase what happened. His chest tightened again and the pain in his arm was starting to overtake him. He reached in the cabinet next to him and pulled a dusty bottle of aspirin. He swallowed three with the last swig of coffee.

Chapter 11

It was obvious Mayor Park did not have the whole story from last night. The coffee and pills were bringing August around to clearer thinking which only made him angrier with himself and sadder over the loss of his friend. He looked up at the bulkhead above the kitchen cabinets. Hanging there was the crucifix off his grandmother's coffin. A woman who after his parents died, did her best to keep him close to God and was so proud when he was ordained. August stared at the cross for a minute, walked over, pulled it off the hook and threw it in the junk drawer. Right now, he didn't need anything reminding him of his past. August turned to the counter by the door and pulled his Glock out of the end drawer, stuck it in the holster in the small of his back, draped the polo over it and walked out of the house.

Chapter 12

All the way down the back walk to the jeep, August was beating himself up for the way he treated Susan. However, the events of last night and her showing up this morning didn't add to his fondness for her. She was an arrogant and stubborn woman, but he was upset with himself for buying in to the local chatter of her lust for gossip and power. He of all people knew better than to make those judgments but he just couldn't see her perspective on city government as anything more than an annoyance. Turning the situation over again in his mind,

"I'll apologize to her later. She isn't going anywhere."

August knew the first thing he had to do today was start his investigation of Fr. Steve's SUV. By this morning it would be down in the local impound lot two blocks over from his office. In his short time as sheriff August checked countless vehicles in the lot after accidents. It was a routine job. Many times, it was easier to discover the cause of the accident in the lot when you could take your time and no one else was hanging over your shoulders trying to get to the answers before you.

This time of a year, late night single car accidents were predictable. Beer cans were often found scattered on the floor of the vehicle or maybe a couple bottles pitched out the window several miles before the accident. It bothered August to think about Steve's vehicle mixed in with the other wrecks. August knew without looking he wasn't going to find any easy clues in this situation. Steve was too cautious of a driver to be drinking or driving careless. August was with Steve more than once coming back from deer hunting trips in blinding snow. Conditions that made even August

71

nervous. But Steve handled the slips and slides like the car was on rails. Steve could probably drive that stretch of Highway 160 with his eyes closed. For him to go off the road meant something went very wrong. Something was not right, and August had his suspicions.

One of the clues that troubled him about Steve's car was the fact it was on the opposite side of the road and there was no evidence of blowouts or skid marks. Based on what he could see from his quick scan last night there were no other vehicles involved. Steve just shouldn't have this kind of a wreck. Steve would never drive at speeds necessary to roll a vehicle in such a flat area. There were times when August would try to get Steve to drive a little faster so they wouldn't miss the morning hatch on their favorite lake. Steve's response was always,

"I prayed for a slow hatch, we're fine. Drink more coffee"

August stopped in the office before going to the impound lot. He was a one-man operation. The budget for the county was too thin to provide for a deputy or office staff. The office was just as he left it at the end of the day on Saturday. He left in a hurry that day planning to spend Sunday fishing up and down the Nassau River. He needed the time away from the job and some of the politics of the county. The all-day rain spoiled those plans and he resisted any desire to return to the office on Sunday to catch up on paperwork.

The annoying message light on the answering machine was flashing like a car turn signal. The faster it flashed, the more messages it contained. August hated that machine. Any machine that demanded his attention as this one did was on his list of things to ignore.

"I might as well get it over with."

Sitting at his desk August pressed the voice mail button. After going through several complaints about noisy parties, dogs, cats and trespassing complaints he got to the heart of the calls. The calls played back oldest to new.

"August, this is Steve, I have Angelina. She is anxious to meet you. I am driving back from Omaha right now. She came in on the afternoon flight right on schedule. She looks just like you thought she might, so she wasn't hard to find. You sending those flowers for her was a nice touch."

The next message was Steve again,

"August, we have a problem…." The call ended.

August played the message over again listening for any background noise. Nothing. Again he played it. Nothing. August let the other messages play.

A local newspaper reporter, Bill Anderson, just doing his job but still snooping, came up next.

"Sheriff Hawk, Bill Anderson, give me a call. I know you and Fr. Steve were good friends, just want to get your reaction. Oh, by the way, sorry about your friend."

The state police headquarters out of Lincoln was the next call.

"Sheriff, we need an accident report when you can. You can fax it over. Also, when you have an I.D. on the other victim we need it for our files."

August reached with his good arm to hit the delete button, but he missed when the pain grabbed him again just like last night. His arm slammed the answering machine sending it to the tile floor and shattering across the office. August followed right behind it. Struggling to get up he made it as far as the door and fell against it blocking entrance to the office.

Chapter 13

Michelle Heights locked the office door behind. Her life in Watercreek was still a work in progress. Since taking the medical examiner job here a year ago, she was still trying to find her place in the community. She is thinking California girl stuck in the middle of farm country might have been more of challenge to bite off. She was also the only professional woman of color in the community.

She couldn't shake the feeling that half the people's opinions were stuck back in the 60's and the other half were just being polite trying to keep an awkward situation even less so. Thank God for the August. He at least talked to her like a professional and the fact they shared a history of service in the Marines didn't hurt. More than once she made August blush with her comments about the two of them. On several occasions she said to August,

"Come on Auggie, let's go out and compare war stories."

Every time she did August managed to change the subject. She knew he was interested in her. The age difference was not the issue even though she was twenty years younger, and for sure it wasn't a race thing. August was just one of those guys you could tell neither of those issues were a concern, but there was something there that just wouldn't let the real August come out.

Michelle had Fr. Steve and the mystery woman from the accident down in her morgue. She knew the condition August was probably in this morning losing his best friend. She was always a little of jealous of Fr. Steve. Now she was feeling guilty about maybe having a better chance for August's attention with Fr. Steve gone. Her plan this morning was to stop by Bill's, grab some coffee and donuts for her and August and see if she could cheer him up a little.

Pickup trucks outnumbered little red sports cars in this town. It wasn't hard for anyone to keep tabs on Michelle's comings and goings. She felt the eyes. The constant surveillance was one of the things that was making it hard to get close to Auggie. She stopped by his house one day to drop off a report and before she got back to her office Mayor Park was on the phone making pleasant conversation but digging as to what she was up to.

"Well, this morning will get everyone talking again." The red Porsche slipped into the reserved spot on the Courthouse west side. The morning sun was still casting the shadow of the building over the lawn, parking spots and across the street to Bill's diner. Inside Bill's is where she felt the most uncomfortable. The diner was the hangout for old white guys sitting around drinking coffee. Every one of them turned toward her as she walked through the door. Not only was she the only woman in the diner, she was also the only African American.

Bill greeted her as she approached the counter,

"Good morning Dr. Heights. You look good this morning. It's nice to see beauty compared to these crusty characters I deal with every day. What can I get for you?"

"Two cups of coffee to go and whatever donuts the Sheriff likes."

"Why do you want to take him anything?"

That comment caught her off guard. She thought Bill and August were friends. More than once she saw Bill, Fr. Steve and August in here swapping fishing and hunting stories like a couple of "good ole boys." What's the deal now?

"You know about the accident last night don't you Bill? Fr. Steve and some poor lady are laying in my morgue right now. I'm sure August is crushed."

"Yeah I know all about that. Too bad for Fr. Steve. August will just need to find a new friend. Here's your coffee and donuts."

Bill motioned for Michelle to move closer over the counter.

"Let me tell you something about August just between you and me. He's not what he seems to be."

Michelle left the diner very confused. Bill was fine until he found out the coffee and doughnuts were for August. She always thought Bill kind of liked her. This was the first time he ever charged her for coffee. He always used to say, "Veterans discount." Coming out of the diner the July heat hit.

The shadow that provided a cool path was growing shorter. The heat on her face made her start to sweat. She felt a little silly worrying about it, but she wanted to look her best for August this morning.

Chapter 14

Susan Park was standing at her office window watching Michelle pull up, run across to the diner then come out with coffee and a bag. She watched as one woman slapped her husband as he spent too much time watching Michelle cross the street. Susan couldn't blame him. She hated to admit it, Michelle was probably the best thing he was going to see all day, next to her of course. Susan timed her exit out to the hall to make it look like she was meeting Michelle by accident. In a sing song practiced political voice, Mayor Park greeted Michelle,

"Good morning Dr. Heights, and how are you this morning. Getting hot out there already isn't it?"

"It is, but I am getting used to it. Thank God for air-conditioning. Have you seen August this morning?"

"Now that you asked, I did. We had a nice conversation this morning over coffee at his house. Poor man, he is just all tore up over Fr. Steve, and the news we learned about August this morning. Well, I am still trying to process all of it." Playing the polite game right back at Susan,

"Madam Mayor, I don't know what you are talking about. Bill just said something like that to me over at the diner."

"Well I am sure August will fill you in. He must be down in his office I saw his jeep on the other side of the Courthouse."

"Thank you, Madam Mayor. You have a good day." Mayor Park watched Michelle move down the hallway. Her tennis shoes making little mouse squeaks on the polished tile floor. Even more puzzled now, Michelle moved a little quicker down the hall to August's office.

Chapter 15

Juggling the coffee and donuts to free up a hand, Michelle turned the knob on the old wooden door and pushed in. The door opened about two inches and then hit a block. A harder push didn't open it any farther but did force the bag of donuts out of her hand. Bending down to pick up the donuts she could see through the crack of the door the body of August laying against the door.

"God damn it Auggie," Michelle shouted as coffee spilled over the floor.

Michelle planted her feet and put her shoulder to the door. This time it was enough that she could get her slim body through the crack and step in. August was laying on the floor. He was unconscious but breathing. Punching in 911 on her cell Michelle connected with the office that was only a couple doors down.

"Get someone to the Sheriff's office immediately, possible heart attack."

Dropping the phone beside August's body she started CPR while tears started to well up. Barking like a drill sergeant,

"Come on Marine. Wake up."

No response from August. She checked for a pulse again. Still very weak. No sign of response from August. She continued the chest compressions. Two paramedics came through the door. Neither one dressed in uniform yet. Michelle continued as they set up to work on August. A crowd started forming outside the Sheriff office door. It didn't take long for Susan to show up and start making all sorts of concerned sounding statements. One of the paramedics pulled Michelle off August and took over with the compressions while the other started an EKG. The siren of the ambulance pulling up echoed through the halls of the Courthouse. Two more paramedics burst through the door with a gurney and immediately started lowering it and spreading the sheets and blankets out.

One of the medics leaned into his shoulder and spoke muffled words to someone on the other end of the radio. Michelle resisted giving orders but instead let them do their work until one of the medics felt August's gun in its usual place in the small of his back. He pulled it out like he had just birthed a child. He looked around to the other medics,

"What do we do with this?"

Michelle jumped in,

"Give it here," her Marine voice was still active.

Without question the medic handed it over. Michelle popped the clip out and racked the slide ejecting the chambered shell she knew would be in there. The medics for one second stopped the process as each guy was shocked by this good-looking lady handling a firearm as easy as she might turn the key in her fancy sportscar. She tucked the gun under her blouse in the tight waistband of her jeans. Now she was in the mood to start giving orders,

"Come on get him moving you're going to lose him if you don't get him on that gurney. Do you have the chopper in-bound?"

One medic nodded a yes to Michelle as he slipped between her and the gurney to take up the head end. Mayor Park stopped Michelle as she followed the medics out of the office. Placing her hand on Michelle's chest,

"Are you sure you want to do this Michelle?"

Grabbing the Mayor's hand with a grip that made Susan wince,

"Now is not the time to come between me and Auggie. I don't know what's going on, but he needs someone on his side right now."

Michelle ran to catch up with the medics. They were closing the doors to the ambulance when Michelle locked on to the shoulder of the paramedic and spun him away from the door. Jumping in and taking the seat next to the attending EMT,

"Let's go, let's go."

Chapter 16

The lead medic kept a check on August's pulse. Michelle held August's other hand no longer as a doctor or a Marine but as a woman. She stroked his hand stopping at every dip in his knuckles. The calluses from years of working with his hands held many stories. She was trying to picture what those might be. His hand was almost as dark as her natural skin up to where his watch would normally be. There, a ring of white, looking like he wrapped his wrist with surgical gauze replaced the watch. The ambulance made a hard-right turn and the force threw Michelle over the top of August. She wanted to linger but jumped back immediately. The medic noticed the embarrassed look on her face and just gave her a slight wink.

When the ambulance reached the helicopter landing pad the chopper was making its final spin around as the pilot judged the wind and how to put it down best. The sound of chopped air vibrated the box of the ambulance. Still unconscious the sound seemed to agitate August. He started thrashing on the gurney. There was a look of fear on his face that Michelle saw over and over in young Marines coming home missing arms, legs and dignity. Beads of sweat were forming on August's forehead.

Chapter 17

The sounds of the helicopter, Michelle's voice and the orders yapped by the first responders sent August deep in an unconscious terror spin. His body knew he was dying and was fighting with the soul that wouldn't let him go unless he answered questions. He was back in the jungle reliving the fire fight all over again.

Chapter 18

Michelle watched as August reached up from the gurney as if he was stroking something in front of him. She'd seen this before. After soldiers went through the most traumatic of situations of their lives, they started reliving them again under anesthesia. Many of them had no recollection of the dream when they woke. She could tell August was deep in a memory.

The medics loaded August into the helicopter. It seemed the closer they got to the helicopter the more agitated August became. Michelle held his hand even tighter and stroked his head. Michelle tried hard to calm him but was pushed out of the way by the medics on the helicopter. One of the flight crew said to Michelle,

"We're sorry Doctor, but there is not enough room for you to go with us. We are taking him to Lincoln Memorial. You can see him there."

One of the local paramedics grabbed Michelle's arm and gently pulled her back.

"Doctor, you know you can't go with them."

"Get me back to my car at the Courthouse," Michelle ordered like she was talking to a private again.

The one paramedic, a veteran himself understood the tone and the urgency of Michelle's order. August was secured in the helicopter. The ambulance left the scene with Michelle riding shotgun and sirens and lights flashing as if they were responding to another call.

Chapter 19

August's mind was swirling from sounds and smells. The antiseptic smell brought him back to the hospital after the attack, but the fuel smell reminded him of the fiery attack on the village. Helicopters flying overhead as the village exploded in flames. Men, women and children running like human torches. His own Marines being shot right in front of him. No warning and no way to defend. The flight crew administered more drugs to keep August calm without putting him over the edge. He grabbed at them in a way they never saw an unconscious man behave. He kept hollering for someone named Galina and yelling about the baby.

Chapter 20

The ambulance dropped Michelle at the Courthouse. She ran to her car hoping that Mayor Park didn't see any of the activity, but she wasn't so lucky. Susan beat her to the parking space and was blocking the driver door.

"So, is he going to live or die?"

"Which would you prefer Mayor? I am guessing either way doesn't matter a whole lot to you." Gesturing toward the gun still in the small of her back,

"Now's not the time to piss me off."

"Doctor, are you threatening me? Again."

"Yes. Now step away from my car."

Mayor Park stepped aside to let Michelle in her car, but not without issuing her own threat.

"You know Doctor, you can be fired from your position just as easily as you were hired. The commissioners that hired you, all owe me favors."

"I am sure they do Mayor."

Michelle backed out never looking and was almost smacked by an old rusty pickup. Susan hollered,

"You should have hit her George, I would've made sure you got a new truck out of the deal."

Chapter 21

The July heat filled the cabin of the helicopter when the doors opened. August felt it as a blast from the fire that was engulfing the village and the surrounding jungle. August was in a different time, place and body. Villagers were running through the jungle. The attackers were picking them off like target practice. He sat up on the gurney and hollered their names. Two flight crew members gently eased him back down.

"Sheriff it's okay, you're at a hospital." August just looked at them. His stare filled with terror showing them clearly, he was not with them.

Chapter 22

Michelle pushed the curtain back surrounding August's bed in the ER. It took her longer to get to the hospital than she wanted. She held back a shocked look as best she could when she saw August hooked to wires and oxygen. He had a scared look on his face and didn't even acknowledge Michelle when she stepped through the curtain.

"August, can you hear me?" He never turned to her.

An ER nurse stepped through the curtain,

"Are you family?"

"No, just a good friend. Can you tell me what's being done? I'm a doctor."

The nurse gave Michelle a once over glance as if she didn't believe her.

"Dr. Vance is evaluating him, but the tests have not come back yet. That look on his face has been there ever since they brought him in. The flight crew said he was going on about a woman and her baby. Maybe that's you. They had to give him some extra meds just to get him out of the helicopter. He won't be talking much the rest of today."

The nurse stepped out but not without giving Michelle another judgmental look. Michelle was tempted to step out and lecture the nurse but let it go. She reached under the covers and found August's rough hand. She moved her hand up his arm pushing the gown back to reveal the snake tattoo. An urge was building inside of her. She knew what she wanted to do, but like a little girl she was so nervous. She looked back through the opening of the curtain. No one was watching. She pulled her hair back with her free hand bent down low to August and kissed him on the forehead.

The curtain flung open scaring Michelle. Standing there was a person Michelle never would have guessed could be connected to August.

Chapter 23

A beautiful Latin woman stood in the opening of the curtain. Michelle judged her maybe twenty-one or two. Taller than Michelle and almost the same skin tone although it was obvious the woman came by hers from the sun. Even as a woman looking at another, Michelle had to admit how beautiful and powerful she seemed, especially for someone so young. Michelle felt the need to break the moment of awkward silence.

"I'm sorry, can I help you? I'm afraid you might have the wrong bed."

The woman spoke with a heavy Latin accent,

"This is Francis Stratton. I know him."

"You are mistaken Miss his name is not Francis. This man is very sick if you would please excuse us."

"This man is Francis Stratton, roll up his gown on his right arm. You will find a snake and tree tattoo. This is Father Francis Stratton. He raped my mother and sent my father to prison, and then gave me this."

She turned away from Michelle and pulled her hair back revealing an ear that was barely hanging on. Pulling up her own sleeves revealing an arm that looked more like fried bacon than an arm.

August opened his eyes just enough to see a woman from his past standing at the foot of his bed. He closed his eyes again and fell back to his unconscious state. Michelle, still holding his hand felt his body tense. She looked down away from the woman hoping to catch August awake. When she turned back, the woman was gone.

Chapter 24

Susan Park couldn't wait to get back to her office following her confrontation with Michelle. The Doctor knew how to get under her skin. She had to let that go for now. Her first order of business was trying to figure out who August really was.

The two of them rarely saw eye to eye but she was one of the people that worked hard to get him elected. She figured she was owed some answers and now she wasn't so sure her efforts were well placed. There were no other candidates for the job that she felt she could manipulate. Surely a man as handsome and mysterious as August would be an easy target for her false charms and good looks.

Those qualities had always worked on other men starting with her father and then all the men who gave her more of the precious information she craved. She was a little disappointed in herself that she didn't get more out of August this morning but maybe it was just bad timing. She hoped she wasn't losing her touch. Susan questioned why one of the firemen at the scene reported to her he witnessed Fr. Steve addressing August like a priest? This was gnawing even deeper at her. Who was August if he wasn't who he presented to the voters and the people of the county?

Susan prided herself on knowing the information in the community and knowing it first. She viewed herself not so much as a politician, but more as a broker of information who found the best source and selling floor for her commodity in the political arena. In high school, she quickly caught on that information, whether it was about someone or something was a valuable commodity. In no time she established herself as the go to girl.

Even with her parents she knew how to manipulate details and stories to her advantage.

As an only child and the product of a struggling marriage, she quickly learned the game of blackmailing. She knew how to wage one parent against the other to get what she wanted. Blackmail was not too harsh of a term. She had pictures of her father and his mistress which she threatened to use if things didn't go her way. Her mother's afternoon escapes from reality on prescription drugs was supported by the countless pill bottles that Susan dug out of the trash.

When her parents eventually split, it was Susan more than the attorneys that mediated the divorce. Of course, she directed that she benefited more than either parent. In Susan's world information could be traded for additional information when needed. She became mayor not for the title or prestige, but rather for the access to evidence she could stash in her bank before anyone else. This new revelation about August made her mad. It was eating at her that she missed this buying opportunity about his background. She was determined to get in on the ground floor before it grew any larger.

All Susan really knew about August was that he came from around Philadelphia. He claimed in his bio that he went to St. Joseph College and then joined the Marines. He worked as a military policeman for years then went back to school for additional studies. All of this had to be true, how else could he pass the FBI background checks needed to take the job?

There was more than one thing that was odd in Susan's eyes. August never carried a cell phone in an era when every kindergarten student has a cell phone. He has no computer skills and no email address. He does everything by paper, mail or fax from his office. His only transportation is that old beat up jeep he drives around. The man doesn't even wear a uniform. Even stranger to Susan, when she cozied up to August's mailman a while back, the only thing she found out was all deliveries were marked occupant.

Susan made her first prying call to the local diocesan office in Lincoln. She said she was an old friend trying to find Fr. August Hawk. No one in the office had ever heard of him. They suggested trying one of the other two dioceses in the state. No luck with either of those. A phone call to the Archdiocese of Philadelphia revealed the same answer. With that call, she did receive the web address of a directory of all priests in the country. She thought, "Now I have him." Searching the list revealed no Fr. August Hawk ever being ordained in the last thirty years.

Susan decided it was time to expand the search. She picked up the phone and called a contact who worked for the FBI. The phone rang once and was immediately answered. Susan's voice bubbled in the best genuine interest she could muster,

"Mary, Susan Park from Watercreek, how are you?"

"Fine Susan, how are things out in the country? Surviving the heat?"

"You are aware Mary that air-conditioning has come to this part of the world…right? We even have stoplights and the roads are paved. We are doing just fine here."

It didn't take much for Susan to turn on the defensive when she suspected even the slightest put down of her state or town. If she was anything, she was loyal to her home place. She knew everyone outside of Watercreek looked at them as sodbusters and hillbillies, an image she was trying hard to eliminate.

Mary couldn't resist poking at Susan. In her estimation, Susan was wasting her talents as the mayor of a small farming town. She should be running a corporation in the city. When their usual sparring finished, Mary asked,

"What can I do for you Susan?"

"Could you research the background of our local Sheriff?"

Mary quickly typed August's name on her screen and without notifying Susan, started recording their conversation.

"Auggie? What for? What could that sweetheart have done to piss you off?"

"I never said he upset me, I just need to know more about him to make me feel comfortable with his handling of some cases."

"Since when did you become a cop Susan? I can tell you without looking him up you are not going to find much to surprise you. I met with him when we did his initial background check. He's a great guy. You should be nicer to him. I can't believe some woman out there in your county hasn't picked him up yet. He would be a good match for you Susan."

The thought knotted Susan's stomach even more. Thinking of her and August as friends was not a direction she wanted to go. She was pretty sure August knew her ultimate agenda and that made him a threat to her assets.

"I will send you the background report Susan, but that is all I can do without an official investigation and this needs to stay between us."

"No, that's okay, don't bother, I probably know everything it's going to say. Thanks for your offer Mary."

Mary hung up the phone, logged the call from Susan and sent a notice up to her superior based on the instructions from the flag on her computer screen.

Susan stepped out of her office into the wall of heat and humidity. It smacked her with the same force as her regret for making the call. Susan never suspected that Mary and August might be friendly or that she even knew him. She knew a bridge was burned. She could be so stupid sometimes.

Chapter 25

Omaha, Nebraska

Dan Faraday, federal marshal in charge of witness protection for the area, sat down in his sparse office. He spent as little time there as necessary. These days it was a place to get free coffee and cool down since the air-conditioner wasn't working at home. The sooner he was transferred out of the Midwest and back to his home in Oregon the happier he would be.

The current assignment wasn't a bad way to finish off his career. This was a laid-back position keeping tabs on his people in mostly rural settings compared to some of the higher traffic areas. He only had a few more years till retirement so he could deal with this for a while longer. Besides, he had a few other irons in the fire that would make retirement a little more comfortable. With coffee in his favorite mug and the morning paper in hand he settled in to catch up on last night's baseball scores. The plan was disturbed by the phone.

"God damn thing, every time I get comfortable, some idiot decides to break my stride."

On the other end of the line,

"Dan, Bob Sission, FBI how are you doing this morning?"

As Dan flipped a page in the sports section only half paying attention to Sission,

"Not bad Bob, what can I do for the FBI?" he continued to scan the page looking for the Royal's score.

"Dan, we received a flagged inquiry this morning about one of your people."

This is not what Dan wanted to hear this early, but these events come up now and then. He flipped to the next page of the paper. Really not giving Sission any more attention than necessary. One of the new secretaries walk past the office glass. He followed her until he almost spilled his coffee. She was more important than the agent on the line.

"Do you have a name for me?"

"Did you hear about the accident last night?"

"No, honestly I just got into my office and haven't even broken open a paper" flipping another page he began to read the ads for fishing boats dreaming about retirement, not the conversation on the phone.

"I guess a local priest was killed in a one vehicle crash last night. He also had a passenger with him, a young lady. She was also killed. We don't have an I.D. on her yet."

"Bill, how does this concern me? I can tell you right now, I have no one under as a priest or any young ladies in my charge. I am too old to keep up with any young charges."

"Dan, it was August Hawk, the caller was looking for?"

Dan felt a rush of heat through his whole body. The air-conditioning seemed as if it quit. His body's reaction was echoed in his voice. The FBI agent could hear the paper being crushed not folded. Dan mouthed into the phone,

"That can't be... It's not time." Then he spoke out loud,

"I'll call you back."

"Thank you, Bill. Keep me informed of any new calls."

Dan cradled the phone with a motion as if he had been delivered news of the death of a loved one. He almost wished that was the case. He had so many things he needed to do right now.

"I wish they had told me this was happening."

Dan knew that what was just placed in motion couldn't be reversed.

Chapter 26

Tuesday, Lincoln, NE

August woke and looked around the room without moving his head. He could feel the heat of morning sun on the side of his face. He knew where he was but not why. He jerked his head in the direction of where he last saw his visitor standing. The only thing there now was a closed door with a hospital escape plan mounted in the center. A quick flip in the other direction he spotted Michelle sleeping, her head about to hit the window sill.

"What the hell is she doing here?"

Pushing up the pain shot through his arm and it was the gasp that woke Michelle.

"August, you're ok, you're in Lincoln Memorial hospital. You had a heart attack."

August lifted his bum arm.

"Your arm isn't broke, but they have it wrapped to keep it from moving any more than necessary. Auggie I was scared for you."

"Where's Angelina?"

"I don't know who you are talking about. I don't know anyone by that name."

"She was here not too long ago. I saw her at the foot of my bed. You talked to her."

"You mean that woman who came in here. She was crazy. She said she knew you and that you raped her mother. She then accused you of burning her and leaving her scarred."

"She's not crazy. I knew her mother and I knew her as a baby. I also know how she was burned. But why was she here. How did she know where I was?"

Michelle was biting her bottom lip when August finished talking. She was trying to forget what the woman said. All she could respond with was,

"You need to get your rest August. You've obviously been hallucinating while you were under. A woman was here but she apparently had the wrong room. They gave you some strong drugs. I am going to check at the nurses' station to see if they can give you anything to help you rest again."

"I don't need anything. I just need my clothes and my gun. If you're not going to believe what I am telling you then keep on walking when you leave."

Michelle reached around her back and pulled the Glock from her waistband.

"Here you old fool, I hope the two of you have fun together."

Laying the gun on the sheets beside his good arm, Michelle turned her back to August not wanting him to see the tears. A night with little sleep and worrying about August was taking its toll. She closed the door behind her, straightened herself up and walked down the hall in her best imitation of nothing wrong.

August rolled over on his good arm and slid the gun under the sheets and squeezed his eyes hard pushing out the tears forming. He was hoping Michelle would never have to learn his past. This changes everything. The door opened, and August was prepared to ask Michelle for forgiveness. Instead a bubbly nurse with a breakfast tray backed through the door.

"Rise and shine Sheriff. I've never had a sheriff as a patient before. Do I call you sheriff or sir or Mr. Sheriff? I don't know but here's your breakfast. Doctors' orders, you have to eat it all."

August tried to keep a disgusted look off his face from her jabbering on. Pulling himself up and wincing at the motion.

"Just call me August. August is fine. Nurse?"

"You can call me Suzie."

"Suzie, glad to meet you. Were you on all night long?"

"Yes sir, I mean yes August. I was here when they brought you in. You were pretty messed up as they say. But you look better now."

"Did I have any visitors through the night?"

"You mean beside the pretty lady that stayed by your side all night? There was another lady who came in while you were down in the ER. She didn't stay long though. Your overnight friend didn't seem to like her sticking around. You're a little devil aren't you having these two young ladies chasing a man your..." She stopped short of finishing what August knew was coming.

"Can you tell me what the other lady looked like?"

"She was a beauty. Tall, silky black hair. Very shapely. She had an accent like a Mexican or Spanish person. She was very rude to the hospital staff I can tell you that...not like your other lady friend."

Chapter 27

After fighting with the doctors, and convincing Nurse Suzie to track down this clothes August checked himself out of the hospital. One call to Stan Farney and a plan was hatched for him to drive to Lincoln and pick up August. August had to get to the heart of what was going on with Fr. Steve and why he was being visited now by Angelina and that wasn't going to happen in a hospital.

Chapter 28

Watercreek, NE

Once back in Watercreek August had the advantage of no one knowing he was back. His first task was retrieving his jeep from the Courthouse and hoping he could do it without anyone noticing. He wasn't lucky enough to escape the patrol of Mayor Park. She watched the jeep pull away from the Courthouse.

"Stupid man. He's going to kill himself before I get the real dirt on him." She grabbed her keys and was out the door having a good idea where he was going.

Chapter 29

August pulled up to the impound lot and logged himself in with a key swipe at the gate. The electric gate struggled to roll itself back. It was like watching an old man pushing a heavy door open. After what seemed like minutes, it was wide enough for August to pass the jeep through. In the rear-view mirror August watched the gate make the same labored journey back to the closed position.

It was no effort to locate Fr. Steve's SUV. There were only two other vehicles in the lot. In the light of day more of the trauma to the vehicle was clear. August stopped the jeep directly in front of the vehicle. He sat there for a few moments. The Fill-N-Go coffee cup in the holder grabbed his attention. August's bloody thumb print was facing him. He reached down and matched his thumb back to the print. His chest tightened and suddenly he felt cold and wet.

Chapter 30

Climbing out of the jeep was harder than getting in. He was starting to regret his decision to leave the hospital. August sat on the edge of the seat before sliding off. He made a grunt like his grandfather did getting up from his chair.

"It's finally happening, getting soft."

The jeep was parked in such a way that it blocked the one security camera's view of his investigation. He didn't need anyone second guessing this investigation. Walking around the wrecked vehicle August immediately started recording in his head all the details of the car. No camera or notepad was necessary. The one thing he had always been blessed with was an exceptional memory. A quality, after the other night, he wished would diminish. There were things he didn't want to remember anymore.

The front of the SUV was bent at a nose dive angle to the ground. The roof over Steve's side was cut and bent back by the jaws and the morning sun spotlighted the blood stains on the deflated airbag dangling out of the steering wheel. Mud and grass covered the entire vehicle giving it more of a camouflage paint job rather than the normal shine that Steve was always proud of.

The driver's door was secured with zip ties. August cut them away and the door swung free towards his legs. The smell of wet carpet, grass, and mud mixed with the humid morning. August carefully pulled back the lifeless air bag to reveal more blood on the steering wheel. The wheel itself was broken and blood was on the jagged edge.

"That must have been what Steve felt in his side."

August bent down to look around the floor boards for any clues also hoping to find Steve's cell phone. No luck with either. The contents of the console were scattered over the floor. Various flavors of breath mints, pens, a rosary and parking passes; none of which added to the story of what might have happened. There was the wrapper for a bouquet of flowers, but August didn't see any flowers at the scene. The flowers must have been mangled in the wreck and probably someone pitched them at the scene. Steve could be a real flirt and charmer when he wanted to be. August figured those flowers were probably meant as much to impress the girl as they were to make her feel comfortable with him for the first time. August made a mental note to check the crash scene for any evidence of flowers.

Walking around the back of the vehicle August found one of the clues he was hoping to find, signs of another vehicle. The rear bumper was crushed. This could only happen if Steve backed into something or if he was rammed from behind. Steve never would have backed into anything with enough force to cause that much damage and a rear bumper does not get crushed like this based on the way Steve's car rolled.

Steve wasn't speeding, he was trying to get away from someone.

Chapter 31

Moving to the other side of the vehicle August tried to open the passenger door. It was wedged tight by the accident. Reaching in to try and get some leverage he ripped his shirt on a piece of metal sticking up through the door. He noticed this same piece of metal already had a piece of cloth stuck to it. The glass from the door was broken and shattered across the floor on the inside. If it broke because of the accident more glass would be on the outside of the vehicle. The seat belt also had a clean cut in it not a jagged cut or tear from an accident. No one would have been in Steve's car without a seatbelt. Steve's was still on when August arrived at the accident scene. The girl wouldn't have been allowed to ride without hers.

The phone didn't seem as important now. What was more important was figuring who forced them off the road and broke out this window pulling the girl through. The first responders all agreed, she was in the field when they arrived. There was no way, based on the injuries August saw the night of the accident that she could have crawled out by herself. There would be no cell phone. Whoever caused this accident mostly likely took Steve's phone before the accident was reported.

Who reported it? And who was in the car that caused the wreck? This was not an accident. The whole incident just turned into a homicide. Someone knew a lot more than August did at this moment. August would need to put this together with the clues he had in front of him.

Now there were four deaths that weighted on his soul. If God was sending him any message that he wanted him back, it wasn't working. August pulled out of the lot and headed toward the morgue where he knew the bodies of the girl and Steve would still be in the hands of the coroner. August was too absorbed in his thoughts to notice Susan's car rounding the corner as he pulled out of the lot.

Chapter 32

Susan followed August as close as she could without being detected as August pulled from the impound lot. She prided herself in being good at following a source, no matter who or what it was. She felt a little rush knowing she was following a professional. Now that she knew she was dealing with more than just a small-town sheriff she was being more careful. August's mystery was her new quest.

Susan watched as August pulled into the community hospital and parked cockeyed in a spot reserved for him. She didn't risk pulling in, that was too obvious. Instead, she decided to pay a visit to the impound lot herself.

"After all, I am the Mayor, they should let me in."

Chapter 33

August walked down the halls of the community hospital. By small town standards this was a top-notch facility. Built only a few years ago it boasted features that made many big city hospitals envious. One of those jewels was the morgue and forensic lab which August, now with tunnel vision, was fixed on. He didn't see the stares of people as he walked through the corridors. Wearing no uniform people not familiar with him thought he was just another visitor. Natives of the area knew better, and they tended to step out of his way as if expecting some wrath to come down, then they whispered in corners as he passed

All of this was lost on August. He was too concerned with running events over in his head. His past and present were colliding with the same trauma as Steve's accident. Pushing through the doors of the morgue, he was greeted by Michelle. She was resting her palms against the exam table as if she was waiting for someone to deal a hand and use the corpse as a gaming table.

"Good morning Auggie, I heard you jumped ship. You're a damn stubborn Marine. If you decide to drop dead, do it in my morgue, you'll make my job easier. I figured I'd be seeing you this morning."

"Good morning Michelle."

Even with a cloud of depression and regret hanging over his head, August couldn't help admitting to himself how good she looked in a lab coat and jeans. Her dark skin against the crisp white lab coat made her look like she just stepped out of a black and white fashion photo. August fantasized more than once about what it would be like to be with a woman like Michelle. On a few occasions, he thought he had mustered the courage to invite her for lunch but then like a scared school boy he wilted. He satisfied himself by rationalizing that there was too much age difference and she was probably looking for someone more exciting than him. August wrestled with apologizing for his actions in the hospital but all he could come up with was,

"Any news for me Michelle?"

"I can tell you three things I know for sure. First, you are the talk of the hospital, hell, probably the whole town by now. The only thing people have not said is that you and I are dating. I also heard the mayor paid you a visit before your trip to the hospital. Should I be jealous Auggie? Is there something you need to share with me?" Both statements made August blush and he could feel that school yard embarrassment that comes when someone calls you out on what you thought were your secret desires. All August could get out of his dry mouth was,

"Let them talk."

Michelle continued, with just a little lighter tone knowing she touched on something.

"Second, neither victim, Fr. Steve or the Jane Doe were drinking."

"Michelle, she is no Jane Doe, although I can't give you a name. Her name is supposed to be Angelina. And, you know as well as I do, Steve would never drink and drive."

"That's good information. But what do you mean supposed to be? Aren't you sure?"

"I don't know what I am sure of right now. I'm working on that. My visit here might help me with a name."

"Well, August, here is a third tidbit, and you probably already suspected, Jane Angelina Doe was not killed by the accident, what you didn't know, was that neither was Fr. Steve. And....this is going to make your investigation even more difficult. He was poisoned. All I can tell you right now is that it was a fast-acting toxin. There was a good chance, from what I can tell from my preliminary autopsy, he might have survived the accident if the poison wasn't in his system. His injuries were severe, but survivable with immediate attention normally administered at the scene or in an ER."

"And the girl, what was the real cause of death?"

"She was suffocated August. She survived the accident, but someone beat this poor girl to make it look like accident injuries, then when she had no fight left, they smothered her and left her out in the rain."

"You're right. I was afraid that was what you were going to tell me. When I examined Steve's vehicle I could tell the seatbelt was sliced, not by the accident, but by someone."

August, was visibly upset by the confirmation of the news he feared.

"And there is one more thing. It's probably just one of those coincidences. One of the firemen that worked the wreck was brought in this morning. His wife found him dead on the back porch. From the reports it looks like he just stepped off the back porch and fell over. I'll keep you posted on that one also."

Michelle noticed the change coming over August before she finished her explanation. She wanted to reach out to him. She took two steps around the exam table that held Fr. Steve and then stopped herself from getting any closer. She figured if she could just touch him that might be enough.

The normally tanned and rugged August was even more pale and soft than when she left him in the hospital. She just wanted to hold him, but she knew August wasn't that kind of guy you walk over and hug.

"August, the woman on the table was supposed to be the woman that visited you right? Who is she August?

August turned and left the morgue without answering Michelle.

Chapter 34

August stepped into the restroom directly across the hall from the lab. The antiseptic smell of the bathroom compared to truck stops and fast food restrooms he was used to stopping in on the road was numbing. He looked around the white tile walls, white waxed floor, polished porcelain fixtures all added to the feeling of loneliness. His heavy breathing echoed off the walls.

August felt like he walked into a room where everything was covered with sheets as if someone was closing a house and moving away. That's what life felt like now. He felt like he had moved away from his life. Alone. The control he thought he gained this morning was gone. The bitter pre-taste of vomit came up his throat. August barely made it to a commode. He dropped to his knees in the cramped bathroom stall. Bent over the commode all he could see in front of him was the image of the stained-glass window from the other night.

A passage from scripture kept pounding in his head, one he repeated over and over in a blazing jungle. "My God, My God, why have you abandoned me?" Just like Jesus in the Garden, August had sudden clarity of what his own destiny was. The difference, unlike Jesus who accepted His outcome, August was going to make sure he avoided what he knew was ahead of him. The mistake he made was the age-old trick of the devil. His new life made him believe evil didn't exist anymore. Here it was right in front of him.

Chapter 35

Susan was successful at gaining entry to the impound lot. Using her influence as mayor plus a promise to send the city crews down to fix some major potholes around the lot didn't hurt her case.

She quickly located Steve's vehicle. Looking around the damaged SUV, she wasn't sure what she was looking for. Tinkering with one of the doors of the SUV and leaning in she spoke out loud,

"I am sure August saw something here that he didn't see last night. I wish I knew what that was. Either Father kept a clean vehicle, or August worked it over pretty good."

Susan knew from Stan the vehicle rolled more than once. It seemed to her that there was not enough blood on either side for such a traumatic accident; but maybe the rain washed much of it off. She rationalized that August apparently took any clues with him he felt were significant. She slammed the driver's door trying to make it latch. It swung back open and knocked her to the ground.

Once she recovered from her embarrassment she looked up and saw what August missed. It could only be seen from this angle. Wedged between the sun visor of the passenger side was a cell phone. It must have lodged up there during the roll and was just missed by the cutting jaws. Knowing she was probably on surveillance, Susan worked her way into the car as if she was trying to secure the door in a different way. Pretending to reach in for support, she grabbed the phone and slipped it down in one quick motion.

This was her prize for the day. Now all she had to hope for was that Fr. Steve, like many, didn't have a passcode. Driving out of the lot, she said goodbye to the owner, gave him a wink that probably made his day, and drove off with her catch safely in her jean pocket.

Chapter 36

Omaha, NE

Faraday locked his office door and made his way through the main lobby of the Federal Marshals office. Few noticed him leaving. Dan was not the kind of guy that attracted attention, which was the way he liked it in his chosen career. He looked like an ordinary guy. Neat, but not overdone. Fit enough, but looking like on any given day, your average forty-year old could out run him.

It was all for show. He believed in keeping up this appearance. He wore clothes that made him look slightly overweight and one step behind fashion. Leaving the office this early in the day was of no interest to anyone. No one except the new marshal recently assigned to the office. Dan didn't notice the marshal following him down the street. The marshal followed Dan almost all the way to his to his car. Once the rookie marshal was confident Dan was in his car, he dialed his phone.

Morning Omaha traffic was brought to a standstill by the explosion. Store windows shattered for a two-block radius. Next to Faraday's car was a clothing store. Manikins were spread out on the street most of them melting from the heat of the car fire. All that remained of Dan's car was a torch of black smoke and orange lips of flame. Car alarms sounded all around drowning thoughts and reactions and adding to the confusion and disorientation. People started running up the street away from the scene. The charging people looked like fall leaves blowing up the street bouncing and stumbling over each other.

The rookie walked down the street as casually as if he had just finished a day's work. Two blocks down he climbed into a waiting SUV and drove opposite of the incoming emergency responder.

Chapter 37

Watercreek, NE

August composed himself in the bathroom and cleaned up at the sink. His pullover shirt had rings of sweat surrounding his neck and arms. The polo shirt fit tight on his biceps forming a collection point for much of the perspiration. He rubbed the serpent and tree tattoo and squeezed it hard with his free hand.

Rage like he hadn't felt in years was still bubbling in his gut. August forgot he was a sheriff and priest. All he wanted was answers that no God or law enforcement agency was going to give him. He was on his own.

August made it out to the jeep without anyone stopping him. The news that Michelle shared with him pounded in his head. August knew the message someone was sending him. There are only three people that could make the connection to his past. One he helped put away in jail. Another was his handler in the marshal office. He ruled Dan out quickly. He trusted him with his life and the third was Steve who was stretched out on Michelle's table. That only left the first. Mumbling to himself,

"so why is Angelina here."

Chapter 38

August turned out of the hospital parking lot and made his way to St. Mary's. He hoped by going through some of Steve's things, maybe a clue would come to him. From there his plan was to run to the accident site to look for Steve's cell. He knew from the voicemail Steve had it with him so if someone didn't take it, then it must be in the field somewhere around the accident. August needed a fresh shirt after the morning's news, and he was finally starting to feel like eating.

He decided to stop by his house since it was on the way to the church. At the house, August couldn't stop the movie running over in his head as he stepped in his house. Visible scenes of Steve's SUV laying on the side. Steve so unresponsive. The girl, whoever she was, laying out along the highway. In a burst of frustration, he kicked over the closest chair, then swept everything off the kitchen counter in broad swing of his arm.

"Damn it, Damn, it" was all he could muster now.

Looking at the mess that now surrounded him that mirrored the mess he felt he made of people's lives as well as his own. August decided to skip the food and go right for the last three cans of beer in the fridge. The demon was in front of him now. He had hidden in plain sight long enough. What haunted him all these years was hesitation.

The events of the last hours and days awakened the fear and regret he carried through the darkness his soul had slipped into. It was obvious two things were coming to an end, his career and his life. At this point he was contemplating the latter. August pulled at the inner corners of his soul for years trying to make sense out of the night's actions so many years ago. As a priest, he was called to protect the souls of others. How was he to do this when he could not protect his soul from himself?

Many nights he sat with a gun in his hand thinking it could all be over in an instant, but something always stopped him from pulling the trigger. He couldn't commit to either his heart or his soul. Both dragged at him. It was easy in this town to hide behind a badge in much the same way he hid behind a collar in the jungle. The witness protection he received from his knowledge of Hector's cartel reinforced the burial of the past. He used it as justification for putting it all behind him. Now, his lack of commitment and hesitation cost the life of Angelina's mother and now the life of his friend and an innocent girl.

The real casualty in the jungle fight was August's soul. He left it in the smoke chocked jungle that night and replaced it with a new one. August joked with himself,

"There are probably few people in the protection program that receive a new soul along with a new identity."

August knew the only way to redeem himself and save others was to start over and trace the path of evidence his soul left behind. August always knew there would come a time when the past would catch him. Now is the time.

August shook himself out of his brooding, went to his bedroom, and threw a few clothes into a mud-stained camo patterned backpack. He unlocked his gun safe and pulled three semi-automatics out. He grabbed shells from the bottom of the safe hoping through teary eyes he was selecting the right ones. He walked out to the jeep, threw his bundle on to the seat, backed up and drove out of town.

Chapter 39

Michelle completed the autopsies on Jane Doe and Fr. Steve. She was convinced of her findings and was anxious to share with August those conclusions. Michelle was still baffled by the results of the tests. She still had the fireman to work up, but his case wasn't nearly as pressing.

The poison that killed Fr. Steve had to be something he encountered earlier in the day. There were no puncture marks from a syringe but there were toxins in his blood she just couldn't identify. Someone went to a lot of work to make it appear they both died from the accident. Michelle checked for toxins as part of a routine exam and then checked again. The idea that Fr. Steve caused the accident out of carelessness was next to impossible.

As the report printed she was gathering her keys to head over to the sheriff's office to bring August up to date.

"Maybe I'll try that cup of coffee again."

Grabbing the report as the last page came out of the printer she stuffed it hurriedly in an official envelope and sealed it with the coroner seal and headed for the Courthouse.

As Michelle pulled away from the hospital lot she was too preoccupied to notice the van that watched and waited for her to leave intent on taking her parking spot next to the lab entrance. Two men, both with ball-caps tipped in such a way that the lot security cameras could not record their face approached the entrance. Each was dressed in white jump suits typical of the cleaning service for the hospital. They walked casually through to the lab. Each carried a tool box and a manual sprayer like the type used for insecticide.

Chapter 40

Stopping just outside of town August switched on a cheap track phone and made a call to Dan Faraday. August hated these things. No answer. He would try him later.

Dust swirled behind the jeep as he headed down a country road forgotten by most people in the county. The heat dried the mud on the road from the rains back to its original khaki dust. Only a couple miles down the road August turned the jeep into a field with a weather-beaten barn on the far end. The tall grass whipped the front of the jeep as he bounced across the open field. He parked beside the barn and made a quick check in the rearview mirror before he stepped out. He looked back again when he set his first foot on the ground and one more time when he reached the man door of the barn.

A new padlock secured a rusty latch holding the door closed. August fished for a key on his ring and finally found the one that fit the lock. Once open, the door hung crooked off a hinge that popped from the dry wood. Inside the only light was what came through the door. The windows were covered from the inside with sheets of plywood tacked around the edges just enough to hold them in place.

August didn't need any light. He knew his way around the barn. He pushed a heavy timber off an L shaped bracket and let if fall under its own weight. He took a few steps and did the same on the opposite end. Twin doors were now free to swing to the outside. When August pushed them, the morning light bounced off an old Ford F-150. The grey hood and roof had spots of rust and droppings from pigeons that somehow always find their way into a barn. August grabbed a broom standing in the corner and swept the dust off the windshield then pitched the broom to the side.

Pushing the double doors completely open he could hear the barn sucking in the fresh air. August walked back to the jeep, popped the hood and removed the battery. He carried the battery back to the truck in the barn and with little effort installed the battery in the old truck. Back out to the jeep, August grabbed the bag he had thrown together and slammed the door on the jeep. Once in the barn he pitched the bag on the seat of the truck, stepped up on the running board and bounced down on the seat. One turn of the key and a little grinding of the engine and the truck came to life. One key click and he was ready to leave another life behind.

Driving out of the barn he stopped the truck in the field, took one last look at the jeep, and drove off with no plan of ever seeing it again. He felt a little better.

Chapter 41

Mayor Park walked into her Courthouse office just in time to watch Michelle slip her little sports car in the space reserved for the county coroner. When Michelle was hired, Susan made sure her parking space was next to the mayors. Susan believed in the saying, *"keep your friends close and enemies closer."* She wanted to make sure she knew when Michelle was in the building.

With one hand on the custom drapes of her office window Susan spoke her opinion to no one,

"She's going to regret that vehicle once a Nebraska winter hits. That is if she is still here then."

There was no hiding the fact that Susan was not a fan of Michelle especially after her incident when they were taking August away. Michelle was another woman of power in this county that Susan might need to deal with some day if she was to reach her goal in state politics. Also, Michelle had a pipeline of information that Susan wished she had. Susan would love to have the relationships Michelle formed so quickly with some of the people in town. Trouble was, Susan didn't know how to be a friend. She never developed that talent.

Watching Michelle make her way up the Courthouse steps she could see some of the local farmers, in town for morning business following her path with desiring eyes. Susan sat down at her desk and started shuffling papers just to look busy in case Michelle or anyone else stopped in.

Chapter 42

Michelle climbed the steps to the west entrance of the Courthouse and made her way to August's office. She checked herself in the reflection of the doors as she walked down the hall. Normally not this vain, but she wanted August to see her at her best. She knew he was hurting and she was hoping she would be the comfort for him. Maybe she could put to rest their disagreement. The cool air of the Courthouse lobby was refreshing, and it made her perk up even more as she approached August's office.

Arriving at the Sheriff Office door she found it locked. A chill ran through as she remembered the last time she couldn't get in. But, this time it was locked.

"I wish he would hire a deputy and take a break. This job really is killing him."

There was no place to leave the report. Michelle felt that August needed the information in the report today. If he would only get with today's technology she could send him a text to meet her. She figured she could get the county radio operator to reach him. She turned in the hall and walked down towards the emergency management office which took her past Mayor Park's door.

Michelle walked past the door at the same time Susan was coming out. The two women met in the doorway. Neither one relinquishing any animosity over the events and encounters of the last two days but both put on a public display of respect.

"Madam Mayor, how are you this morning?"

"Fine, not so hot yet which is okay. What brings you around this morning?"

"I have some reports for Auggie," she used his nick name knowing it would get under Susan's skin a little. It did the trick. Susan was not always good at hiding her reaction. She turned on a cold tone.

"I am sure the old goat is in his office."

"No, I just came from there he must be out already. The office is locked."

"I would be happy to give them to him."

Michelle was not ready for that play by Susan. Susan won that round. There was no reason not to leave the reports in her hands. After all, the report was sealed with the coroner's seal and the mayor was a public official. If she protested, that would just raise more suspicion and she knew Susan would direct that towards August.

"Okay, just make sure when he comes in you give the envelope to him." With a sarcastic and sloppy salute,

"No problem, I will make it my duty."

Michelle didn't miss the sarcasm but what could she do. There was nothing on the outside of the envelope except the last four digits of Steve's social security number, Michelle's method of tracking cases and the other name, Jane Doe. The two women parted, and Susan returned to her desk, placing the report in her top drawer.

As soon as the door closed it hit her. She pulled it back out. There right in front of her was a number she had not tried. The last four digits of Steve's social. Pulling the cell from her purse, she typed in the 7296, the phone came alive with missed messages, texts, and emails. Susan slumped back in her chair like the "cat that swallowed the canary."

Michelle, back in her car, was overwhelmed by the heat built up already in her little sports car. She pulled the latch that activated the roof and felt the heat lift off her as the convertible folded back. She wished it was that easy to free herself of the doom she felt turning the envelope over to Susan. If there was any way to avoid it, she would have.

Chapter 43

With the roof secure, Michelle drove to August's house. She figured maybe she would be lucky enough to catch him home. As least there they would be on safe territory with no Susan sticking her nose in. Maybe she could be a little freer to tell August how she really felt in the safety of his house. It would also give him a chance to be more open about his visitor.

She crossed the highway and silently marveled at how one could see from one end of this town to the other.

"What have I gotten myself into taking this position?"

Her home in California was cooler and more scenic. But then, August wasn't in California. When she met with the search committee for the new Medical Examiner, August was part of the interviewing team. She figured if the county had a sheriff that looked like him; it couldn't be all bad.

Pulling up to August's house it was clear that he was not there either. No sign of the old jeep and the house was closed up. August liked the fresh air, if he was home all the windows would have been open.

Knowing his lack of home security, she also knew the door would probably be unlocked.

"What's the harm," she figured.

"We're friends and after all, I am just checking up on him, I am a doctor."

Pulling the screen door back she pushed the heavy ornate wood door in. It took some effort on her part and she made a less than graceful entrance in to the kitchen. Her first thought when she regained her dignity was that she never knew August to keep such a disheveled house. There were chairs out of place around the table and one even toppled over.

Michelle searched the house to reassure herself that August was not there and that he was okay. She sat the chairs back up and picked up the magazines and other items laying on the floor. She found a notepad and pen on a counter and left a note for August to call her when he came home. She resisted the urge to add anything more personal on the note. She felt like a little girl writing a note to the neighbor boy. She chased the feelings away. *"Marines don't gush."*

Getting into her car she almost sat on it. On the open car seat was a small delicate flower.

Chapter 44

Michelle, her hands shaking, pulled a rubber glove from the supply she kept in her car along with an evidence bag. Barely able to pull a glove on one hand she settled for that being enough. With the gloved hand, she carefully picked up the flower and dropped it into the evidence bag and placed it in her console and drove back to the Courthouse. She was hoping who ever placed this in her car was dumb enough to leave prints behind.

Michelle immediately knew the message and now the manner of Fr. Steve's death and maybe even the unexplained death of the volunteer fireman.

"I need to retrieve the report. This is all bigger than a small-town scandal of a priest and a mistress. "Where the hell is Auggie?"

Chapter 45

August drove most of the day. He made sure he stayed off the main interstates. Instead, he drove through the small towns and grain stops located on back highways. He stopped in one small town that reminded him of Watercreek.

The Courthouse sat in the middle of a town square. Businesses surrounded the square most of them looking like "mom and pop" operations. He parked the truck outside a bakery, one of the businesses that surrounded the Courthouse. The old ford's door creaked as he pushed it open and it caught the attention of a crow picking up spilled grain in the middle of the street.

August was hoping the bakery had some coffee as he hadn't see any place for miles that looked like a good coffee stop, and maybe just maybe a few doughnuts this late in the day. He was planning on being farther away from Watercreek by now, but the downside of back roads traveling is hay wagons and slow-moving tractors.

The smell of fresh bread filled the shop and stirred memories of August's grandmother's house. That's when things were easy. He and his grandpap would go fishing in the morning and come home to fresh bread and plenty of homemade strawberry jam and coffee. He'd been hooked on coffee ever since.

They would all sit around drinking coffee till the pot was empty and listen to grandpap telling stories from his years in the Marines. It was usually on one of those mornings grandma would pull out the weekly letter from his folks and they would all try to picture the exotic places his parents were in.

The bakery was set up with a long glass display case with rows of empty pastry trays. A few notices were taped to the glass. One printed on yellow paper warned people to not let their dogs jump up to the counter. But, right under it was a note, "Don't forget to ask for our daily doggie treats."

There was also a notice of a tractor pull coming up on the weekend down at the local fairgrounds. August remembered the first time he ever heard of a "tractor pull," he couldn't believe how far away from the jungles that phrase had taken him.

A few sugar doughnuts were left near the cash register. As he was eying them up a stubby little woman came out from the back, her gray hair, wrapped tight with a white cloth, was trying to escape around the edges. Her apron was partially covering a cowboy style shirt with the sleeves rolled up. When she leaned forward on the counter August could tell by her tanned and muscular arms she did more than just work in the bakery.

"What can I get you honey? We don't have a whole lot left this afternoon, but I have some things in the back I was just packing up to put out for day old. I got some bear claws and jelly doughnuts back there and a few loaves of bread."

August, sticking his finger on top of the glass counter like a little kid picking out penny candy said,

"I'll take those two sugar doughnuts right there, and it would sure be great if you had some coffee to go with those."

"I don't have any coffee right now sweetie, but if you can wait just a minute, I can put a pot on. I could use some myself."

"That would be great, I need to make a few phone calls outside. I'll be right back."

"I'll be waiting for you hun."

August stepped out on the side walk and looked across the street at the Courthouse. Unlike his Courthouse, this one was bathed in shade from big old maple trees surrounding the building. The grounds were manicured like a golf course and a few sprinklers were spitting across the lawn.

August walked down to the truck and kicked the tires just for the heck of it. He opened the creaking door and reached across the seat to his backpack and pulled out the track phone. He sat on the edge of the seat with his legs hanging over the side and focused on the sprinklers after dialing up Dan

Faraday's number again. It rang seven times, just like last time, no answer. It made August a little nervous.

He started wondering if he could start over in this little place and just not tell anybody. No handler, no Fr. Steve, Michelle or Susan Park. He shut the phone off and slipped off the truck seat and slammed the door shut. This time it scared the same crow and it took off to the top of the nearest light pole and glared down at August. It was as if the crow was the only creature that saw him as a stranger in town.

When he went back in the bakery he could smell the fresh coffee. That made him feel better. He walked back up to the cash register which made the same woman magically appear from the back room. She carried with her a mug of coffee and plate with the two sugar doughnuts.

"Here you go sweetie, you look like a man that needs a good cup of coffee. You have a seat over there and I'll bring it over to you."

At the corner of the bakery were small round tables, not much bigger than diner plates themselves. Each one had delicate chairs with decorative wire backs that August wasn't so sure would even hold him, but he figured he would trust them. Pulling the chair away he straddled the seat and carefully lowered himself down. The bakery worker noticed his hesitation.

"You don't have to worry hun, the guys we get in here, if they were going to break, they would have done it a long time ago."

She placed the mug and doughnuts on the table which left little room for anything else.

"My name is Gabby, not my real name though that's just what I've been called since I was a little kid because people say I talk a lot. I really don't talk that much it just seems like my mouth wants to start before I really want to say something. Do you know what I mean?"

August just smiled and looked up at her as he took the first sip of coffee.

"You enjoy sweetie, there's plenty of coffee in the back you just knock on the counter there and I'll bring you some more."

August took a bite out of a doughnut and could taste his grandmothers baking all over again. Looking out the big display window, he was surprised to see a line of SUVs and pickups all with heavily tinted windows passing through the main street of town. August was glad they were going in the opposite direction from him. That many black SUVs hiding their occupants can only mean trouble for somebody.

August finished the mug of coffee quick and it only made him want more. The doughnuts would give him the sugar and carb rush he needed to keep driving again and the caffeine would carry him the rest of the way. He decided to take Gabby up on her offer of more coffee and walked up to the counter and sheepishly tapped on the register like Gabby said to do.

This time when Gabby came out she seemed nervous that he was at the counter. She made sure she pulled the curtain separating the work room from the front of the store.

"You need more coffee? I'll bring it to you, you just go sit down."

It seemed more like an order than a friendly coaxing, but August complied. Gabby came out as soon as he was seated, again making sure the curtain was pulled tight. She brought the pot over to August and poured it with a shaking hand.

"Are you alright Gabby?"

"Oh yes, I must have had too much coffee myself, it does that too me."

"I've been drinking coffee since I was a little kid, I don't think it has much effect on me anymore. How much do I owe you?

"Oh, you don't owe me nothing. I was going to throw those doughnuts out for the old crow out there and the coffee I needed. Can I ask you a favor?"

 "Depends Gabby, you know I am not from here."

Sticking her hands in her jeans pockets under her apron she spilled out a nervous request,

"You look like a man that might have a tattoo."

"I do, but why do you ask?"

"I kind of have a thing for tattoos, could I see it?"

August rolled up his sleeve to reveal the snake working around the tree trunk.

"I didn't expect that. That is beautiful."

As quickly as she requested to see the tattoo, that's how fast she left August side.

"I hope you pass through here again," she hollered back to him as she parted the curtain and slipped into the back. As soon as Gabby stepped through the curtain a man in a flowery shirt chewing on a cigar grabbed her arm. He ordered in a dry hacksaw voice,

"So, tell me about the tattoo."

Gabby described as best she could what it looked like and the description seemed to satisfy him. He looked through a crack in the fold of the curtain and watched August go out the door. Once he was sure August was gone, he turned back to Gabby and slit her throat with one quick slice. Gabby fell to the floor, her eyes wide open staring at the ceiling and her apron turning red with the blood.

He stood at the front door and watched August pull away and travel down the road in the opposite direction the SUVs had earlier passed. He stepped outside looked up at the crow still perched in the tree. He tossed the stub of his cigar out in the middle of the street and turned back into the bakery. The crow swooped down and picked at the cigar stub, grabbed it in his beak and took off.

Chapter 46

Watercreek, NE

The rookie marshal was dropped off outside of Watercreek at the north edge of town just beyond The View Café. The SUV turned around and drove away. The rookie by this time had shed his suit and tie and now looked more like one of the locals rather than a government man. He wore a broken-in ball cap, blue jeans with a ring from a can of snuff, and boots that showed hard use. His blue cotton western style shirt with the sleeves rolled halfway up hung outside of his jeans which did a good job of hiding the gun tucked in his waistband and gave full view of the Nebraska Huskers logo on the chest of the t-shirt.

He walked from his drop off into the main part of town. He blended in so well that several people passing by on the highway waved to him thinking they knew him. He gave a friendly wave back and by the time he reached the turn of the century hotel in downtown he was one of the locals.

No one suspected the nature of his visit or the way their community would soon be changed by his visit. The rookie checked in at the front desk using the name Bob Saine, a representative for the state agricultural office. The woman registering him blushed when he winked at her as he finished signing in. She informed him his bags had arrived earlier and they were already in his room. She wished him a pleasant stay in Watercreek.

Once in his room, Saine pushed back the curtains revealing a perfect view of the main section of the downtown as well as a direct view of the Courthouse. Across the street from the Courthouse he spotted what looked like a mom and pop café on Main Street.

"That will be a good place for lunch and to listen in on some of the local gossip."

He closed the curtains, stretched out on the bed and flipped on the TV to watch the local farm and market reports and baseball scores, information he would need to fill his conversations later.

Chapter 47

Wednesday, St. Louis, MO

August arrived at his destination close to dawn. He stopped along the way and caught up on some sleep. He found a busy truck stop just outside St. Louis where he could hide the pickup among all the other trucks and where it wouldn't be so unusual to see a guy sleeping in his truck. He wished he had taken a few extra doughnuts from Gabby, but she seemed in a hurry to get rid of him. Probably closing time for her.

Now that it was getting close to dawn his final goal was an old Victorian house located in the suburbs of St. Louis. It was built in a time when excess was the rule; more rooms, windows and doors than anyone would ever need. August lived in the house years ago along with other young men studying to be Jesuit priests. The community grew up around the place leaving the house a small retreat in the heart of two stall garages and backyard swimming pools.

August parked the truck down the street and switched the Nebraska plates to Missouri plates so that it wouldn't create too much suspicion parked in the neighborhood.

No one was out at this hour. A heavy morning fog had dropped on the neighborhood. The kind of fog that turns the light cast by streetlights into pyramids of light and headlights into laser beams cutting through cotton. The fog was a good indication of how humid it was going to be later. A few houses had lights on in the kitchens and he could see in the closest house a woman pouring a cup of coffee in front of a window. A man came up behind her and kissed her gently on the neck.

August turned away.

He pulled out his track phone and made one more attempt to reach Dan Faraday. No Answer. August was even more concerned. This hour of the morning there was no reason for him not answering his phone, he should be home in bed like the rest of the world. He had already used the phone too many times.

August dropped the phone to the cement, crushed it with his boots and kicked it in a storm drain. Reaching in to the truck he pulled an old black cassock out of his gear bag. The cassock was shaped by the wrinkles from being stashed away for years. Throwing it on over his t-shirt and jeans, he was proud that it still fit, however it didn't fit his soul as easily. Tugging at the collar he squirmed as if someone put a hangman's noose around his neck.

"Maybe this is what Judas felt like after collecting his thirty pieces."

August reached back in his bag and pulled out one the handguns and slid it underneath the cassock. August struggled to move toward the old house at the end of the street. All he could muster at this point was to stand and look at it. After a few minutes, he was finally able to make his legs move. The birds were waking up and their songs were distracting his thoughts. A few dogs barked as he passed their yards. He silently thanked them for the distraction.

As he moved closer to the house he looked like one of the priests from the house out for an early morning walk. He felt a bit of relief knowing anyone who might see him would never even suspect he was a sheriff or his ugly past. August smiled to himself and let out a muffled laugh, until Sunday night, no one would have suspected him being a priest.

August found his way into the back of the house and climbed over the garden wall as he did many times returning after curfew. Once on the other side he entered a world that was separated from the rest of the life. It was a place that was hidden from all the dangers and problems on the other side of the wall.

Chapter 48

Father Demetrius finished his morning prayer and closed his breviary and carefully placed a ribbon marker for his midday prayers later. He smoothed the ribbon out with age spotted hands. He sat for a couple minutes just breathing in and out and listening to the sound of his own breaths.

The small chapel inside the house was an intimate place for everyone living there. It gave them a place to meditate and pray with no expectation of talking to anyone. Demetrius was the most frequent utilizer of the space. He liked to imagine when the room was someone's living room years ago. Families must have sat around and shared stories in the pre-TV and radio days.

There were two stained glass windows in the room left over when many homes boasted this type of glass. The windows added a chapel feel. There was one of these windows on the east wall the other the west. Demetrius enjoyed being in the room when the sun was rising or setting and being bathed in the colored light of the windows. It lifted his spirits and helped him forget some of the things that haunted his soul. There were things he prayed every day to forget, but they seemed to be his constant companions.

Demetrius pulled himself up using the back of one of the chairs in front of him. The years and the experiences of his earlier days were beginning to catch up with him. A priest for almost fifty years, Demetrius had a special position in the community. It was his task to assist in the training of the men that came to the religious life from unusual situations. Some had careers in previous lives which many people would never suspect leading to the priesthood. He prayed for these men each day often spending hours by himself in his room or here in the make shift chapel. Many candidates did not become priests, but Demetrius never lost contact with them. Some left his charge to be scholars. Others sought out the missions, and then there were those who took the mission of following Gods calling to the extreme.

Demetrius was aware of the seduction of evil that was strong on these souls. Those who went out with the most zeal and purpose were the ones tempted the most. Demetrius knew those temptations and he remembered how weak he was when tempted.

Prayer was exhausting for him. His conversations with God sometimes became so animated his whole body moved and communicated a language of its own. He told his brother priests this was why he preferred to pray alone. It drained him of his physical strength and he knew it was distracting to others. Leaving the cool air of the chapel he stepped into the morning heat of the garden. It was to be another hot, humid day. Too hot to wear black, but he just couldn't shake tradition. It reminded him of what he was called to be and how far he strayed.

Finding his favorite shade spot to watch the garden birds he saw a priest walking towards him from the far end of the garden. With the cassock synched tight around the waist there was no mistaking the silhouette formed against the backlight of the sun. His broad shoulders and erect stature gave him away immediately. Demetrius stood up and walked as quickly as old legs would take him to greet his student and friend. The two men exchanged manly hugs in the middle of the garden. They slapped each other hard on the backs and sat down on the nearest bench to start a flood of catching up.

Chapter 49

From the garden bench Demetrius guided August into the house through the nineteenth century heavy wooden door nicked from years of moving furniture in and out. Demetrius directed him like he was a visitor that had never been there, cautioning him not to trip up on the threshold. August out of habit lifted his foot but still caught the heel of his boot as he passed over. He didn't wear boots the last time he crossed this threshold.

Climbing the stairs, they creaked with the weight of two souls afraid to speak what was really on their minds. Demetrius in front lifted his cassock with one hand and steadied his frame with the other on the railing. August stayed several steps back feeling his way up the steps wearing a cassock again.

Once in Demetrius's room, the two men relaxed and dropped the performance they put on for anyone who might have seen them together.

"Francis," Demetrius using August real name,

"Would you like coffee?"

"That's would be great Father, it was a long drive."

"Francis, I'm not going to lie I am excited by your visit, but I am curious why you are here. I haven't seen or heard from you in years. The last I knew, you gave up the cassock."

August heard a tone of disgust in Demetrius's statement.

"Yes and no. My life has not been my own since South America."

Demetrius focusing on making coffee thankful for the distraction of not looking directly at August while he answers him,

"That doesn't surprise me. My own time on that continent was the most challenging to my vocation. Jesuits have a history to either erase or live up to in the jungles."

August figured he would get right to the heart of why he returned to the house.

"What do you know of my time there Demetrius?"

"Not much. I know when you came back to us, you were a different man. I could see your soul was no longer your own and the passion for the gospel was gone. You are one of the many I pray for every day."

"I was a chaplain to a group of Marines whose mission was to work with the locals to eradicate one of the most powerful drug lords. He enslaved the women and children and utilized many of the men as his own private army. My mission was to take care of the spiritual needs of the Marines while they worked their assignment. I spent much of my free time trying to develop relations with the village people and gain their trust. I loved the people Father. It wasn't hard for me to see why my parents spent so much time with them. But I couldn't save them.

I was face to face with the devil in his hell. I know now my cowardice and hesitation stopped me. I had the gun in my hand, but I couldn't pull the trigger. I could have put an end to it all. The evil that plagued them would have been gone. It was as if my soul was sucked from me and I was no longer Father Francis. I didn't recognize myself for the revenge and anger that surrounded me.

An FBI agent came to see me. It appears I was the only one left that could identify Hector. They wanted to hide me for my own protection. I figured God was finished with me at this point. I had allowed the death of woman and let her baby fall into the hands of Hector. I didn't feel like a priest anymore anyway. Once I testified against Hector they gave me a new name, a new location and that has been my life up until this week.

It was a couple years after that when I pressured the FBI to find they baby. They tracked her down with a family in Chile. I knew that once Hector was in prison, there would be no one to care for the baby I watched him steal. I felt so guilty that I have been supporting her ever since. I've been sending money to my handler for him to pass on to the family. She had no idea it was me that was helping. It was Fr. Steve, the only person outside of my handler that knew who I was, who insisted that I see her and somehow arranged for her to come up to the States.

The problem. The woman that Fr. Steve had in his car was not the baby I have been helping. The fire did too much damage to the baby for her to look so beautiful. When I saw her body, I knew I had been duped all these years. Now they are both dead and I am no closer to understanding why this imposter was killed in such a violent way along with Steve.

I close my eyes now and I see every dead Marine, Galina, the baby, even the dog that licked my wounds. I feel like I am standing in the middle of the underworld alone.

The devil is back Demetrius.

He is hunting me.

He knows who I am."

Chapter 50

Watercreek, NE

Susan, flushed with the excitement of cracking Fr. Steve's phone decided she needed to treat herself. It was lunch time across at Bill's. That was where everyone went to get news of the day or share their latest version of the town gossip. Bill's was a great place for any politician to hang out.

Susan was busting to share what she found and give the people the impression that she was one step ahead of their Sheriff. Walking into Bill's diner the drone of the over the door air-conditioner blocked the bubbling sound of the conversations until she was a few feet beyond the door. Fried onions, hamburger grease and left-over bacon scent filled the air.

All eyes turned towards Susan. Numerous greetings of "Madam Mayor" went out to her as she searched for her favorite table. She walked to the middle of the dinner with a strut like a fashion runway performance as she dodged tables and pulled out chairs. She unbuttoned the top button of her blouse fanning herself showing off how hot it was. She also knew, with that little gesture, she had just secured a few more votes. Everything for a reason.

More than one local came over to complain or compliment. Like any good politician she could change her sincerity based on the needs or the person addressing her. Finally, one asked the question she was waiting for.

"Have you seen the Sheriff this morning? I hear he is back in town"

"No, I haven't, and I have some new information about the accident with Fr. Steve that I wanted to give him. It is so tragic that he had that young girl with him and our Sheriff knew her. I just can't figure out what those two were up to."

Right there Susan knew she planted the seeds of a field of gossip. Her constituents pushed for more information and Susan faked embarrassment for sharing too much. She sipped her coffee and eyed a new face in town sitting at the opposite end of the diner, a fit man in a loose cotton shirt and jeans. His ball cap sitting on the table beside him seemed to have some official insignia.

Her next job as mayor, and as a woman was to get to know this stranger. Finishing her coffee Susan made her way past the stranger just close enough that he had to notice her. She even backed into his table when another patron wanted to squeeze past.

If he didn't notice her now, then he must be dead.

Chapter 51

Michelle made it back to the Courthouse as most of the staff was heading out for lunch. Her hope was that Susan was not in her office, she didn't want another confrontation. Walking into the mayor's office she was greeted by Anna, the niece of the mayor, hired as summer office help.

In the most professional voice she could muster and keeping August on her mind,

"Good afternoon, my name is Michelle," not seeing a need to throw the doctor title.

"I know who you are, what can I do for you Doctor? The mayor is not in now."

"I dropped an envelope off earlier for the Mayor and I need to add something to it."

Anna was smarter than Michelle gave her credit. Anna stepped out from behind the desk and in front of the door as Michelle moved towards the closed double doors.

"If you would just get the envelope, I will be out of your hair."

"I am sorry, I can't do that my Aunt, I mean the Mayor would be upset with me."

Without thinking about it, Michelle grabbed Anna's shoulders and pushed her clear of the doors. Anna hit her head on the back of a file cabinet and slumped to the floor. Michelle knew as a doctor she should be concerned, but as a woman she was more concerned with Auggie than some little teenager.

Pushing into Susan's office, she hurriedly and with no real plan, started checking every drawer and shelf. She was quickly rewarded finding the envelope in Susan top desk drawer. The seal was not broken.

Running out of the office she saw the young girl struggling to get up from the floor. She made a quick assessment that she was going to be okay and walked as fast as she could away from the office without attracting attention. Glancing to her right she caught a view of Susan returning up the steps of the Courthouse. Michelle left the building from the opposite entrance.

Chapter 52

Saine noticed the Mayor eyeing him and she was not being discreet about it. She was going to be an easy target. These small-town politicians were the easiest to manipulate. It wasn't hard for him to pick up on Susan's sarcasm listening to her talk about the Sheriff to the other patrons of the diner. Saine overheard a few of the locals talking about the death of their beloved pastor and how awful it was that the young girl was with him. The Mayor's gossip sprouted quickly and by the time it arrived close to Saine's table they had the priest and Sheriff using the girl as their personal sex toy. Saine knew the real story. He thought to himself if he was right, when the events of the next couple of days are over, and they play out the way he thinks they will, these same people are going to feel guilty about what they are saying now.

The bigger prize was too great to risk spoiling their gossiping fun. He thought the Mayor was coming over to introduce herself but all she did was brush past his table. He knew what she was up to. He performed this dance many time himself.

"I'll just let her lead."

Chapter 53

St. Louis, MO

August left Fr. Demetrius' room and walked down a hallway that hadn't changed since his days as a student. He knew where this path was taking him but he was powerless to stop it. Before he wanted he found himself at the doors of the chapel.

Pulling open the one side of wooden double doors he stepped into a space flooded with colors from the windows. A hint of incense was still in the air from morning Mass. He walked in and took a seat close to the back of the chapel. He didn't genuflect as he really wasn't sure why he was in there or if he even believed in what was supposed to be present.

This was a first. He hadn't been alone in a chapel since the jungle. He leaned back on the wooden backed chair and felt the pressure of the gun still in his waistband as it pressed against his back. He reached through his cassock and freed the Glock from his back and laid it in his lap. August looked down at the Glock and started to curse the gun.

"Why have you followed me here? You have taken everything away from me and given me nothing. When I needed you, you weren't there. My life was better without you."

August realized he was not cursing the gun. He was yelling at God. He slumped off the chair and fell to his knees on the floor. The gun slid from his lap and landed alongside him. August fell into a deep meditation, reliving again the years of dark nights and torments. Exhausted from little sleep and his draining confession to Demetrius, he fell asleep, his head in his arms slumped over the chair in front of him.

Chapter 54

Watercreek, NE

Susan walked into her office and found Anna sitting at her desk, her blouse ripped and a large bruise showing through what was perfect makeup. Susan's reaction was first to comfort the young girl, thinking the worse. Susan started to gather everything to rush her to the hospital, but Anna mentioned one name that stopped her.

"It was that doctor lady. She came by for an envelope she gave you. I tried to stop her, but she shoved me out of the way."

Susan's anger, as usual, told her what to do. This confirmed to her that August and Michelle were working together to cover something up. After making sure her niece was okay despite her bruises. She calmed her down and instructed her not to mention this attack. Her niece was reluctant but figured Aunt Susan knew best.

"Just tell your parents you had a bad fall in the office and I sent you home." If no one knew about this situation, Susan would be able to work better behind the scenes. If it was reported, then she might never get her hands back on the report. Michelle had just upped the game and Susan was ready to play.

This was her sport now.

Chapter 55

Michelle returned to her office in the hospital. One of the pleasures of being a one-person office is that no one knows when you come and go. She didn't need to explain her absence.

"Maybe this is why Auggie likes to work alone."

She couldn't get the mayor's niece off her mind. She didn't want to be that physical and was honestly shocked at her own strength. The phone on Michelle's desk flashed a message.

"Michelle, its Susan. I am sure you are aware my assistant had a nasty fall in the office. Young girls can be so clumsy sometimes." Susan paused just long enough to let the suggestion sink in.

"We really need to get together sometime and talk over our mutual interests. You have a good day."

Michelle pitched the phone on to the desk. Michelle knew exactly what Susan was doing. She now had something to hold over her head. Her next move had to be the winning hand. There was no turning back now. She knew enough not to be in debt to Susan and she had just given her everything she needed.

"Where's Auggie?" Michelle yelled at an empty office.

Opening the sealed autopsy report she went quickly to the Jane Doe file. There had to be something else here that she missed. Two people murdered, and now a missing sheriff. Who was this girl that August gave a name to? She came with no I.D. or history, but August and Fr. Steve knew her. Michelle left her office and walked down to the morgue to re-examine "Jane Angelina Doe's" body for anything that she might have missed.

Walking into the morgue, she flicked the lights as she had done hundreds of times. A flash of light and heat knocked her back against the door. She fell against the steel door cold against her back in sharp contrast to the heat on her face. The air itself seemed to burn and she knew her only hope was to gain enough strength to open the door from her position on the floor. To stand would be to place her head in the cloud of flames bubbling above her. The vacuum created by the fire was too strong for her. The door was swelling shut and fighting her.

"So this is how it ends."

Chapter 56

The door pushed in and a hand grabbed Michelle by her blouse collar and pulled her around the door and out into the hallway. At the same time air rushed in and fueled the fire even more. Fire alarms blared up and down the corridor. The rescuer immediately began to check Michelle for injuries and burns. Michelle got a glimpse of her savior but didn't recognize him. He looked like any one of the farmers that came through the hospital.

In seconds Michelle was surrounded by doctors and nurses. They rushed Michelle from the hall to the emergency room. She thrashed her head back and forth on the gurney trying to spot her savior. He was not among the group that was now tending to her.

The automatic sprinklers in the lab activated but not until the bodies of Fr. Steve and "Jane" were cremated from the intense heat.

Chapter 57

Bob Saine walked north towards uptown against the flow of fire trucks, emergency vehicles and curiosity seekers. Back in to the hotel, the siren mounted on top of the hotel was still blowing to call the volunteer fire company to the hospital. He gave another wink to the same desk clerk that checked him in and caught the elevator to his top floor room.

His visit to the morgue had been more eventful than he anticipated and came close to revealing his cover. Saine sat down in an overstuffed chair tucked in the corner, analyzed the cheap painting of a barn in a winter cornfield hung on the opposite wall, put his feet up on the bed and fell asleep.

Chapter 58

St. Louis, MO

When August woke, the sun was coming from the other side of the chapel. His dreams and meditations had taken him to his own personal hell and back. He sensed that he was not alone. He reached for his gun and it wasn't there. A hand cupped his shoulder and he turned with clenched fists to find Demetrius behind him.

Demetrius stepped back to avoid what the thought was going to be a swing of punches. He reached out to calm Francis.

"Francis, I've been here with you. I heard you talking in your exhaustion. I know what you are going through. I can't believe I am saying this, especially to you but there is a necessary sin some of us must commit to fulfill our appointed role in this life. Judas knew it, Pilot felt it, so did Herod, and so did I."

Handing August the gun, "Here is your sword. It is the only power that can free you from the demon that is chasing you. Your battle is with this devil man, not God…free yourself Francis."

Demetrius walked out of the chapel, but not before handing August a folded paper. The paper had seen better times. It was covered with water spots, mud and what looked like smeared blood. August unfolded the paper. The writing on the inside was a style he had not seen since he was a boy.

"Dear Francis, Your father and I miss you so much. We have taken a day away from the village to have a little picnic and cool down around a lake in the jungle. The local Jesuit priest, Fr. Demetrius told us of this little hideaway. I hope you are behaving for your grandparents. They tell me you

are doing well in school. The young children here are eager to learn just like you. When we get home..."

The letter stopped there. No love mom and dad. No signature. Just more dirt. August knew what the ending meant. His parent's death was starting to make sense now.

August carefully folded the letter following the original creases. He reverently slid it in the pocket in his T-shirt under the cassock. He stood up and took the cassock off and let it drop to the floor. August walked out of the chapel stepping on the cassock not over it.

Chapter 59

Demetrius, back in his room made a call. The call went to a voice mail. Demetrius punched in a series of numbers,

"He knows everything. I delivered his parents to your father. I am not delivering him. I fulfilled my end years ago, now leave me alone. You should be prepared for him to kill you."

Demetrius cradled the phone as he watched August walk down the lane and exit the house and garden. Once he was certain August was away from the grounds, Demetrius walked over to the desk that occupied almost one whole side of the room. He pulled the high-backed chair away from the desk and sat down and stared at the mementos on the desk. There were trinkets from various assignments scattered across the front of the desk. Some took the shape of little dolls, others were pictures of him surrounded by smiling parishioners of various backgrounds. He sat in one spot for over an hour.

From a spot reserved for his breviary he pulled the book out and recited the midday prayers to himself. Finally, when he was finished and confident that most of the men had left the building for the day, he pulled from the bottom drawer something he had been saving for the day he knew was coming. He placed the muzzle under his chin, and with little thought, pulled the trigger into a new life.

Chapter 60

Watercreek, NE

News of the explosion at the hospital reached the mayor's office minutes after the alarms were sounded. Rushing to her car, Susan forgot all about her concerns over Michelle, August and the "other woman" as the town was already starting to call her. Pulling up to the main gate of the hospital she could see the activity at the far end. She was waved through as an official person with no need to check credentials. She thought,

"That never gets old."

She handed her car off to one of the local volunteer firemen in the exchange he told her it was the morgue that went up in flames. She knew it was wrong to wish Michelle ill but then, she didn't wish her any happiness either. After asking if there were any casualties or injuries she was told only three. The ME was taken to the ER for smoke and minor burns, the other two were already dead, and the fire just finalized things.

Susan turned around, retrieved her car, and returned to her office. There had to be something on that phone that would answer all that was going on and she was going to find out.

Chapter 61

Thursday

Michelle turned over in her hospital bed. When she did she was shocked to see August standing between her and the east window of the room. Through groggy morning eyes there was little doubt who was standing beside her. August reached over and pushed her hair out of her face. Even in her weak state from the fumes, she felt a rush run through her. She had been waiting for such a touch. She wanted to reach up and touch his hand, but she just let him lead where this might be going.

"Good morning"

"Morning August"

"You look like hell Marine."

"That's what a fire will do to you."

"You look like hell yourself Marine."

"That's what a night of driving will do to you."

"August, what's going on? I've been to your house. It was a mess. That's not like you. I found clues since we last talked but I am afraid the fire has taken care of much of that. I am convinced none of this was an accident, but all of the evidence is gone."

"Michelle, all you need to do now is rest. I'll share with you what's going on when its time. Right now, rest, I'll need your help soon. Count on it. Now, I need to go home and follow up on some things. I wanted to make sure you were okay. I'll be back later."

August reached over and touched the back of his hand against Michelle's face. He didn't know why he did it. Her skin was cool to the touch. He snapped his hand back as quickly as he placed it. August, red faced, stepped out of the room into the hallway.

"Good morning Sheriff. We've missed you."

"Morning to you to Madame Mayor."

August walked down the hall without looking back.

Susan looked back hoping she would catch August trying to get a look at her. Michelle was snuggling down in the bed with close thoughts of Auggie when the door opened. Knowing it was August returning she put on her best smile and pulled up in bed.

"Good morning Michelle."

Michelle felt fear like her first day at Paris Island with an angry gunnery sergeant in her face telling her how worthless she was.

"Were you expecting someone else to come through the door. Oh, you poor girl to see me, you must be so disappointed."

Chapter 62

Saine made his way out of the hotel and cut an angle across the street to the diner side of Main Street. It was still early in the morning and the traffic lights were set to flash yellow with the lack of traffic. A few pickups were parked diagonal against the curb and the smell of fried food and fresh bread drifted out of the diner.

By this morning, many downtown regulars already knew Bob. He was quickly accepted as one of them. It didn't take long for the stories to circulate that he was the one that pulled Michelle to safety. Walking into the diner, more than one table invited him to sit with them. He graciously accepted the invitation of one group and quickly jumped in the main topics of weather, price of corn for this summer and who was going to be the next governor.

Bob dug a little deeper with the stories about the Sheriff, the priest and this young girl. He also listened to the gossip of the Sheriff being an ex-priest. Bob put on his best Catholic act and it wasn't long before he was embraced as an adopted son of Watercreek. He left the diner with more than one invitation to go fishing on the weekend and even one local encouraging him to date his daughter.

After breakfast, Saine walked down Main Street opposite from the hotel and diner. No one took notice of his scrutiny of how the buildings were connected. Some of the buildings, being over hundred years old, were taller than the new stores stuck between them which were only one or two levels tall. Saine stopped on the last corner of the business district. There was an old clothing store that still had signs painted on the brick for Oshkosh overalls but the signs in the display windows advertised the handmade crafts that now occupied the old suit racks. On the other side of the street was a shoe store and a hardware store. In front of the hardware store was a guy he met at the diner. They exchanged a few greetings and the gentleman invited Saine back to the diner for lunch.

Looking back up Main Street towards his hotel Saine acknowledged to himself that they certainly picked the perfect spot. Most likely the event would happen any day now. He would be ready. All his planning and practice led up to this intersection of events. From what he knew about the people and the information he was able to gather; the day of the priest's funeral would be a perfect setup.

A few people honked and waved at Saine as he crossed the street and walked back in the direction of the hotel. His walk took him past the Courthouse and he decided to stop in and pay the mayor a visit. He figured by the way she acted in the diner, she would be happy to see him.

Chapter 63

It was hard for August to walk back into his house. When he left, he planned on never coming back. His time with Demetrius and time spent in the chapel, told him what he must do. If he was ever going to move forward and shake the past, he had to return. Watercreek is where his final judgment would take place.

But, life was different. Different from how he ever imagined it would turn out.

August flipped the switch on the coffee maker and without thinking grabbed the carafe and stuck it under the faucet to fill. He stepped to the side and reached for the junk drawer to pull out an opener for the coffee can. Reaching in he grabbed the base of the crucifix he had pitched in two days ago. Pulling it out it stuck to his hand as if it was glued. He stared at the image on the cross and was only broken from its hypnotic hold by the carafe overflowing in the sink. August threw the cross back in the drawer and shut off the water.

He left the kitchen and unpacked his small bag and headed out of the house. August figured the diner would have coffee on, plus he didn't feel like cooking his own breakfast anyway.

Chapter 64

Susan was getting settled into her office for the morning when Anna knocked on the door to announce she had a visitor.

"Who is it?"

"I don't know, but I've seen him around town. He was over at the diner this morning when I stopped in for coffee. He's cute."

Susan straightened herself up a little and shuffled some papers on her desk to look busier than she was.

"Give me a minute and bring him in." Anna closed the door behind her to address the stranger in the outer office.

"The Mayor will be ready in a minute."

Bob Saine noticed the bruise on Anna's face.

"Looks like you lost the fight."

"No, fell over my chair. Clumsy me."

"We've all done it." In the middle of the sentence; the Mayor opened the door and acted surprised to see Bob Saine standing in her office. In a mayor voice,

"Won't you come into my office, Mr., I am afraid I don't know your name."

"Bob Saine, State Agriculture Department."

The mayor closed the door behind her as she followed Bob into her office but not without signaling to Anna not to disturb her.

Chapter 65

August walked into the diner and was greeted in unison by everyone. Some called him sheriff, others hollered out his name. George Stash who had been the postmaster in town for years called August over to his table. August politely declined with a wave and pulled out a chair at his usual table, one that gave a view up and down Main Street.

It was obvious the tone was different in the diner. His normal greeting was reminiscent of when he was a kid and a priest would walk into the classroom and every student would greet the priest in one voice. When August sat down he was immediately greeted by Bill, who made it his job to work every table.

"I am surprised to see you Auggie. The last time I saw you they were taking you out on a stretcher. Are you sure you should be here?"

"Why Bill? Are you afraid your cooking will finish the job?'

"I can only hope. You're a stubborn old man. Your usual?"

"Just eggs and toast."

"I'll get you some coffee."

August could detect a coldness in Bill but chalked it up to maybe he was just off to a bad start for the morning. August looked over the crowd. He watched more than a few faces turn away when he looked up and caught them off guard staring at him. From his table August looked out the window and scrutinized people coming and going from the Courthouse. It was his spot to observe the heart of the city and still enjoy a cup of coffee.

Bill all but threw the order on the table. The toast slid off the plate.

"Hey Bill if I wanted the food thrown at me I'd give it to our Mayor. Bill wiped his hands on his apron,

"Whatever," and walked back into the kitchen.

August watched him walk away trying to figure out this attitude change with him. Finishing the last bite, he looked up to catch the mayor and a man walking out of the Courthouse together. He didn't recognize the man but everyone passing them seemed to know him. The stranger shook the hands of a couple of the guys and a few of the women walking by looked back to admire him when they figured he wasn't looking. The mayor seemed to know him well as she gave him a quick hug as they parted.

August watched him walk down the steps and turned in the direction of the hotel. August motioned for Bill to come over.

"Bill do you know that guy?" Pointing to the man in ball cap walking down the street. Pouring August fresh coffee,

"Sure, name is Bob Saine, he's been coming in here the past few days. Someone said he is from the state Ag department."

August followed him from his spot in the diner until Saine passed beyond the window. He was troubled by his familiar look but figured it would come to him the less he thought about it. August took the last drink of coffee, placed a few dollars on the table for a tip and walked out of the diner acknowledging a few folks on the way out.

Out on the sidewalk, August looked down the street in the direction of the stranger but didn't see him. August turned in the opposite direction to start a walk down Main Street. He enjoyed walking the streets of a town he was challenged to protect. But this morning was different. He walked from memory of the curbs and crossings. He didn't respond to the greetings of people he passed. More than one person asked how he was feeling with no response back from him.

He was rolling over in his head the images and events of the last two days. In his mind he was passing jungle huts and walking on washed out roads. He was lost in the images of the battered Angelina replacement, the exhausted body of Michelle this morning and Steve's car perched precariously on the edge of the ditch and his final request before dying. August stepped off a curb without looking and was almost hit by a driver who had the green light. The driver was ready to yell his opinion at the pedestrian until he realized who it was. August crossed over to the opposite side of the street and started his walk back towards the Courthouse and his office.

Chapter 66

Susan stepped back into her office after telling Bob Saine goodbye. In a moment of slight giddiness, she slowly closed the door behind her briefly resting her hand against the door as it glided back. Susan agreed to have dinner with Saine later. She felt pretty good about herself. Her obvious ability to attract the attention of the men she wanted was verified by Saine's visit. The fact he was younger than her was even more of a confidence booster. If he was who he said he was, this could be a very advantageous night out.

She was anxious to find out more about his purpose for being here and how it could add to her political coffers. He alluded to a big event that would happen in Watercreek. If the state was involved, she wanted to be the first to know about it. Susan was floating on an ego cloud that wasn't going to burst for a long time. This morning and the events of the last two days did not seem as important as they were an hour ago.

Chapter 67

Michelle convinced the attending doctor she was okay. She promised to take it easy the rest of the day. She collected her clothes which still smelled like burnt oil and rotten eggs from the fumes of the fire. She made her way to her office in the hospital hoping that she still had a change of clothes in the closet. Someone was thoughtful enough to bring her purse down from her office. She fished through it to grab her pass key and phone. She was fearful that someone had already gone through it. Her fears were relieved when she found the flower she collected still in the evidence bag.

Once in her office, Michelle dressed in fresh clothes making her feel better. She needed to see August again and was hoping to make a better impression than earlier, but impressions would need to wait, she needed to track down where that flower came from. Fortunate for Michelle, the lab, next to the morgue was not destroyed by the fire. Breaking her promise to take it easy Michelle went straight to the lab where she could research additional information concerning the flower.

Chapter 68

Her suspicions about the flower was correct. The flower was one of the deadliest. Known as the queen of poisons, or the wolfsbane. A victim can only last several hours after touching the flower. All Steve would have had to do was pick up the flower or brush against it with any bare skin and the poison would start acting. No trace of injection. No rashes or cuts. Very few medical examiners would know what to look for. Michelle's course in natural toxins taken on a dare that was never meant to pay off was coming through now.

Someone knew that Michelle would know what this flower was cable of. Someone placed that flower to help Michelle or to silence her. Whoever it was, left fingerprints on her head rest. She was hoping the FBI could identify their owner. Michelle drove away from the hospital with plans of a quick shower and return to the lab and wait for the results of the blood she took from Fr. Steve and the girl when they were first brought in.

Driving down Main Street to her apartment at the opposite end of town, she passed August walking back up the street. Fortunately, he was turned away from the street as she passed. Michelle could not shake the feeling that she was being watched. For the first time, she regretted having such a standout car.

Chapter 69

August made it back to the Courthouse lawn. He stopped to talk with a couple of the regulars that parked themselves on the bench under the shade of the reported oldest tree in town. The same guys met there every morning. They were better than any security camera, they knew the comings and goings of most people from their vantage point.

"Morning Sheriff," came from Greg Kotts who used to own the local shoe store. He knew almost everyone in town and probably fit most with their first shoes. His other friends joined in, each commenting on weather, heat and shame of what happened with Fr. Steve and asked how August was feeling. August joked with them.

"You guys behaving?"

"We are Sheriff, volunteered Greg.

"How are you feeling Sheriff? Heard you had a little scare?

"I am fine guys. You know what it's like. All part of getting older."

"Guess you have a deputy helping you out now?" George said as he poked the other guys while all three broke into laugh at a secret joke between them.

"What are you talking about?"

"We could see you checking out Fr. Steve's car the other day. We have a perfect view of the impound lot from here. Just after you left, Mayor Susan followed you. She must have been making sure you didn't miss anything."

August didn't allow his anger to show. He made a joke that if she wanted his job too, it was hers.

"See you guys later; stop in if you want some coffee, I'll have the pot on."

Once inside, August picked up a package sitting at his door, most likely his new phone system. He unlocked the door and pitched the package on his desk. The room was thick with heat and he turned the dial on the air conditioner with a quick anger flick of the wrist. The hum from the machine helped to distract his thoughts and quieted the ringing in his ears from elevated pressure and anger.

"What the hell was she doing fishing around Steve's car?"

His first reaction was to march down to her office; fortunately, the cool air started to calm him down and began to come up with a plan how to handle the revelation about Susan. He cut open the package and plugged in his new phone and answering machine. Once he had a dial tone, he made a call to Dan Faraday. No answer.

From his hotel room, Saine watched Michelle's red Porsche drive up Main Street. He also followed August as he stopped to talk with the old men on the bench and kept an eye on the Mayor's assistant walking across the street to the diner for her morning break.

Saine made a call to St. Mary's parish office to ask what time Fr. Steve's funeral was scheduled. An automated phone menu gave the Mass times along with the update of Fr. Steve's funeral at 10:00AM Friday.

Chapter 70

Michelle felt better now after a shower and was at least able to take a breath without smelling the fumes from the fire. She replayed in her head the flash from the light switch and the rolling clouds of fire above her head. The bodies of Fr. Steve and the young girl bothered her. She respected their bodies. In her mind, they died a second horrible death. She felt like the devil himself was in the morgue with her. At the thought of that, a chill ran through her. The man that saved her. She wished she knew his name. He seemed to be there just when she needed saved and then he was gone.

Michelle was anxious to get back to work. She rushed around the apartment gathering things she felt she would need. Without giving much thought, she pulled a semi-automatic handgun from her dresser drawer and racked the slide back putting a shell in the chamber. She forgot how good and empowering that action felt. She slipped it in her small handbag, brewed a cup of coffee, got in her car and drove back to her hospital office.

Again, the feeling of being followed haunted Michelle. She was paying more attention to the rear-view mirrors than what was ahead of her. Ever since the morning at August's house, she felt she had a shadow. She decided to change her route to the hospital. This path would take a little longer, but she would be able to see behind her for a greater distance. A little bit of her Marine training was kicking in again. She was starting to appreciate the flatness of the town and some of the unobstructed views.

There was a lot of traffic on the main road through town. The July heat was reaching its peak for the day and many of the farmers and their families were coming in to town to escape the heat in the fields. They would finish their work later in the day working from headlights and illuminated barnyards. The kids were being dropped off at the swim park not far from the hospital while the parents spent time at the Wal-Mart at the opposite end of town.

Michelle pulled into the hospital lot and parked in her assigned slot. In her office, she immediately went to her computer to see if there were any results from the blood test. Nothing. She figured it was early yet, these things take time.

She placed a call to August to see if she could accompany him to Fr. Steve's funeral. She wanted to be as close to him as she could. He was going to need support. She thought about him standing at her bed this morning. She wished she would have had the courage and strength to pull him next to her. For now, she replayed his touch and that would need to be enough until this was all over.

August's office phone rang several times then went to voice mail. It was not his voice, just the canned voice that comes with the machine. She was hoping to at least hear his voice. She would try later. Walking out of her office, she left her computer open to her email and walked down to the morgue to inspect the damage.

Chapter 71

Susan Park instructed Anna to make reservations for her and a friend at the hotel restaurant for 6:00. Susan left her office and the Courthouse by way of August's office. She made a point of clicking her heels hard on the ceramic floor. She loved the sound of authority it gave as it echoed up and down the hall. She wanted people to know she was coming.

Susan opened August office door just as he was slamming the phone down. She never let go of the door knob. Instead she leaned into the office like one would lean over a cliff to look down.

"Easy August, I hear you're going through phones faster than you are careers."

August didn't react. He didn't even want to look in her direction for fear he would disclose what he knew of her sneaking around.

"I just wanted you to know that Michelle and I had a nice talk this morning. We are planning lunch together soon. I thought you would like to know your two favorite girls have been getting along great in your absence."

Susan straightened herself back into the hall and gently closed the door. She knew what was just shared with August would be the start of the wedge between he and Michelle.

"God, I'm good," she thought. She knew how to make these situations work. She greeted a few Watercreek citizens as she passed by with a political smile. She let her heels tap even harder as she walked away and at the same time dialed up her favorite stylist for an afternoon appointment. She had confidence in how the evening was going to go with Bob Saine, but a little insurance never hurt.

Chapter 72

August wasn't back in town more than a half a day and already Susan had been the source of repeated bouts of anger. How could one woman generate so much confusion and hatred? Mumbling to himself,

"Maybe I should just tell her the whole story. She might leave well enough alone at that point. What was with her digging around the impound lot? There is nothing there that would be of any value to her. She and Michelle, together, that doesn't make any sense either, but she was going into Michelle's hospital room earlier."

August sat in his chair and let the cold air from the air-conditioner blow down the back of his neck. He decided to place a call to the alternate number for Dan Feraday. He was instructed to use the alternate if he lost contact with Dan for more than two days in a row. August tapped out the numbers on the new office phone and waited for the request of an access code. After entering it, he could hear the call being channeled through the various networks and security before it went to a regular ring. While waiting, August was looking around the office as if he was seeing it for the last time.

Chapter 73

The cell on Saine's nightstand started to vibrate across the stand. He knew who was calling. He answered,

"Marshal Steve Lassco, how can I help you?"

"Marshal, August Hawk. I am trying to locate Marshal Dan Feraday. The number I just dialed I was instructed to call when I was not able to reach him."

Saine got up from his chair and looked out the hotel in the direction of the Courthouse directly across the street. He could see August's window and imagined him pacing back and forth in his office while he talked.

"August, I am afraid I have some bad news. Dan Faraday was killed on Monday. The details of which I can't share with you, you understand, but how can I help you?"

There was a long pause and Saine could hear Hawk cussing in a whisper and he figured the thump must have been August kicking something over.

"Is something wrong?"

August got back on the line and cleared his throat.

"Yes. I have no doubt my identity has been compromised, and there are some individuals in my community, that I don't know. As sheriff, I know pretty much everyone. There is one person who disturbs me. He's been hanging around downtown and with some of the people I associate with, but no one seems to know where he came from. He is staying at the hotel and goes by the name of Bob Saine. He is telling people he is from the State Agriculture Department."

"Sheriff...August, let us check him out and I will get back to you. I understand you operate without a cell."

"Yes and no, I need to get a new one. Just call back on my office number."

"Don't worry August, we will find out who he is. Now what are the other events happening that have you concerned?"

August brought the new marshal up to date including his time as a priest and all that went on in the jungle. When he was finished he felt like he had confessed his soul to a stranger. For the first time he felt some freedom. It was different than sharing his story with Demetrius or Father Steve. He also knew he had shared more than the marshal had asked for. He said his good byes and hung up.

Bob Saine clicked the phone off. Smiled at himself in the mirror and walked into the bathroom to shower for his date with Susan.

Chapter 74

Michelle walked back into the office depressed after reviewing the damage done to the morgue. A state of the art facility that was reduced to charred walls, melted plastic and bent steel tables. The heat, intense as it was, destroyed everything. The corpses, what was left of them, were removed and sent to the funeral home for processing.

She returned to her office and sat down at her desk and started flipping through emails and reports that were starting to back up. Most of the emails were deleted without even giving them much attention. The further down the list she started to delete with increasing apathy which matched her overall mood right now. Moving so quickly, she almost eliminated the email that bounced her back to the present.

The report she was waiting for contained news she never expected. She couldn't believe the results of fingerprint analysis. She hit the print button and grabbed the report from the printer, deleted the email from her account, then placed the report in her office safe. She picked up her purse, forgetting about the weight of the automatic. She was glad she had it after what she just read. Now she knew, she could only trust herself and August.

Michelle locked the door behind her and walked to her car. Her plan was to drive around town to clear her head and maybe stop at the local bar restaurant at the end of town. She was convincing herself that a few cold beers and a steak was what she needed.

Chapter 75

The sun was starting to cast long shadows over Main Street as Susan pulled into the parking lot of the hotel. The grand structure, one of the few remaining in town from days when corn and railroads ruled the territory, cast a shadow over a full parking lot. Susan stepped out of her car and checked herself one last time in the windows. She felt good about herself. Her tight leather skirt with a crisp white blouse tucked in showed all her finest features. She opted for flats as she didn't want to tower over her date. Most of the time she enjoyed the feeling of power over men, but for some reason, this man made her feel different.

The two agreed to meet in the lobby, which was really Susan's preference. She wanted as many people as possible to see her with this new man. She knew many women in town would jump at the opportunity to be with a man of such mystery and good looks. She also felt if he had any state contacts, she wanted to be seen on his arm as often as possible.

Susan looked up to catch Saine coming down the long flight of stairs. He was dressed in jeans, polished cowboy boots and a pale blue dress shirt contrasting with his deep bronze skin. This was the first time she saw him without his ball cap, his thick black hair was casually slicked back. She thought a model could not have looked any more inviting. As they walked out of the lobby, more than one person followed what looked like a celebrity couple out on a date.

Susan arranged for a table in the middle of the hotel dining room. She didn't want anyone to miss the opportunity of seeing the two of them together. Normally on an occasion like this she would be up and down working the room. Instead, Saine's charm kept her glued to her chair. When dinner was over the couple made their way to Susan's car.

A light breeze was adding a little cooling to the parking lot. They pulled out and headed down Main Street. Bob didn't take his eyes off Susan, and he knew she was aware of his stare.

Chapter 76

August closed the office and decided to walk home. The evening was cooling off which was unusual for a Nebraska July evening. He just couldn't get in his jeep one more time. Too much time was spent inside, and he needed fresh air.

Walking down the Courthouse steps he caught a glimpse of Susan and Bob Saine across the street in the hotel parking lot. That confirmed to him that the two of them were getting better acquainted. He couldn't let her get under his skin anymore today. He had to focus on Fr. Steve's funeral tomorrow. He was delivering the eulogy and he hadn't even begun to think about what to say. Just the fact of going inside a church let alone getting on the altar was scary enough. It would be the first time in years looking back at a congregation. August also had the state police breathing down his neck for answers to the accident. So far, he had been able to keep the fact it was no accident between he and Michelle. That wasn't going to be the case for long.

The conversation with Marshal Lassco bothered him. The fact that Dan was dead scared him. It seemed Lassco was too free with that information. Was Faradays' death connected with what is going on in Watercreek? He trusted Dan, but it took years to build that trust. This new guy seems too casual. He didn't know why he spilled his guts to him like a little kid caught in a lie, now he regretted giving so much information. August decided to skip the walk home in favor of walking just a little farther to the bar at the end of town. It was always good for cold beer and good food, maybe that is what he needed to start getting himself back on track.

Chapter 77

Six large boxy SUV's traveled north on highway 75 towards Watercreek. Inside, every available seat was occupied. The vehicles pulled off the hard top onto a gravel road snaking a path between two corn fields. Dust followed behind the last vehicle giving the fleet the look of a rocket trailing smoke from liftoff.

Once parked, the parade of vehicles was met by several men in a clearing. These men directed each SUV to a designated parking place in the field. A windsock blew from the barn at the end of the parking field. A twin-engine plane made several circles around the barn judging wind and speed then touched down on a makeshift runway cut out of the end of the cornfield.

The pilot and copilot climbed out of the plane and walked toward the men standing along side their SUV's. The pilot was immediately recognized by the men and they acknowledge the authority of the pilot as the two approached them. Each man started to straighten up a little. Removing a black silk flight jacket the pilot tossed it to the copilot and with arms stretched out mimicking the plane, the pilot took in the cooling breeze coming across the open field. Angelina Fuentes pulled off a ball cap and let her long black hair drop and fly in the breeze and then signaled the lead driver of the convoy to follow her into the barn.

A man was standing at the door of the barn dressed in a tropical shirt and the stub of cigar in his mouth. As Angelina stepped through the door she stopped and acknowledged him. He reached for her hand and gently kissed it. The rest of the group broke up and made ready to sleep beside their vehicles.

Chapter 78

Michelle pulled into the small bar at the end of town. It was the local evening hangout in the same way the diner was during the day. It was the place to go for cold beer, fried food, and many other things that weren't good for you but made you feel better. She parked her car up the street to avoid the bumps and scraps that often happened in these parking lots. People that knew her soon learned she took better care of her car than she did herself.

Walking down the street to the entrance she was already tasting the beer and a steak as rare as they allowed it to come out of the kitchen. Stopping at the door, Michelle looked behind her as if she'd left something at the car, still finding it hard to shake the feeling she was not alone. The sun was drawing shades down on the fields she could see from this edge of town. No place to hide there, turning the other direction, she could see far up the main highway, all clear there. She decided to let her guard down a little and enjoy the evening.

Walking through the door the noise of multiple TVs playing the evening Kansas City Royal's baseball game along with just as many opinions flying rose from the crowd. Michelle lost herself in the crowd and found a table deep in the back.

Chapter 79

Driving down the highway Susan didn't share with Saine where they were heading. She wanted one more opportunity for as many people as possible to see her with this good-looking guy. She wasn't sure if it was her imagination or the few drinks she had at the hotel, but he was even better looking now than before dinner.

Once they arrived at the bar, Susan couldn't wait to get out and walk through the tavern door with Bob on her arm. Every good politician lives for the moments when the crowds' eyes are on them. This was going to be the end of a great day. And, if she was picking up Bob's hints it was going to be an even better night.

Unlike Michelle, Susan parked her car as close to the entrance as she could find. She wanted everyone coming in to see that the Mayor was in the house. Bob opened the door for her as she walked through. She started greeting people at tables as soon as she walked in. Susan pitched a few comments to the patrons about the Royals game and the heat of the day. Each comment led to an introduction of Bob Saine. He made an immediate impression on every individual. Some he already knew from his mornings at Bill's. Susan introduced him to the ladies on purpose. She could sense their envy.

Susan was back in her high school days as she walked through the bar. Now she was the girl that all the others wanted to be. This was going even better than she thought.

Michelle watched as Susan worked her way through the crowd. She lost her appetite for anything when she saw Susan and Bob. Susan eventually made her way close to Michelle and the minute she spotted her she pushed her way through the crowd, dragging Saine by the arm.

"Michelle, it is so good to see you out and about after your near-death experience. I would like you to meet Bob Saine, he is the man who saved your life yesterday you know."

Susan reached out and gave Michelle a big political hug. At that same time, August walked into the bar in time to see Susan and Michelle hug like old friends and Bob Saine standing alongside taking it all in. Looking over Susan's shoulder Michelle saw August standing in the door and there was no doubting the look of disgust on his face.

"I must be going I am sorry," Michelle said pushing herself away from Susan.

"Don't be silly stay and have a drink with us. You can't run off from the man who saved you."

It was no use on Michelle's part to argue. Susan had her and August was already out the door before they sat down.

Chapter 80

August slumped down the steps of the bar back on to the sidewalk running parallel to the highway. The walk back up the highway towards the Courthouse was a lonelier one than the walk down. August knew now he lost the allegiance of Michelle and what Susan had alluded to earlier in the day was true. He was in no mood to think about Fr. Steve's eulogy and he was half planning at this point to not even show up. Steve would understand. The more he let himself entertain that thought, the better the idea sounded.

By the time he reached the Courthouse and turned down the street to his house, he'd made up his mind that he wasn't even going. August's mind raced the whole walk. How much easier things would have been if he had been killed in the jungle. He would be hailed as a martyr in a class of many of the Jesuit brothers that had gone before him. He wouldn't have this survivor's guilt that plagued him every day. His struggles with women would be over. He had accepted celibacy as a way of life a vow he maintained even not living the life of a priest.

Angelina's mother was his first temptation. She was a beautiful woman, but one that needed cared for in a way that was beyond his ability. Michelle, who he lobbied for the role of medical examiner was another issue. He had to admit there were others that might have been smarter and more experienced, but maybe not as attractive. Susan, who he battled with constantly. She was a thorn in almost everyone's side, but no one wanted to admit it. But he knew, she liked him, and he respected her, she just always needed to be the first to know the news. She was politician twenty-four hours a day. And little Angelina, her of all people fell victim to his curse. Every woman he felt close to or respected was turning on him or died.

Never seeing Angelina since the night in the jungle he couldn't imagine what the girl's life would have been like. He never wanted to meet her after she was taken away from him, but he had stayed in touch with those who cared for her and raised her after Hector was jailed. Dan Faraday made sure money made its way to her and that his identity remained a secret. Now he realized he had been duped all these years. It wasn't until Steve pushed the issue of the two of them meeting that he finally gave in. He knew that Steve felt this would help bring him back to the priesthood, but August knew different. His salvation was with a gun not with his prayers or meeting this baby after all these years. He tried the prayers for too many years. At least carrying a gun, he had been able to provide some help for Angelina in a way he never could have afforded as a priest. God didn't want him now anyway. August wasn't sure right now if that was a good thing or a bad thing.

August walked through the screen door but caught it just before it slammed for some reason remembering the number of times his grandmother yelled at him to not let the door slam in their old house. If she was alive, she would be one more woman he would be disappointing.

Walking to the refrigerator he pulled out a beer and a sleeve of crackers out of the cupboard. He sat at his table until the crackers and beer were gone. He turned the air conditioner to the max cold climbed into bed and pulled the covers over his head and for some reason could not stop reciting the "Hail Mary" prayer over and over in his head. He finally fell asleep covered up like a kid hiding from a thunderstorm.

Chapter 81

Friday

When the morning sun shone enough light to move around, Angelina rallied leaders to the barn. She moved with cold detachment from everyone present. She didn't make eye contact with anyone. She regarded the men with no more concern than the bales of hay stacked in the corner. Each man in front of her was only a tool. Men knew they were expendable by her and gave her a wide path, both in her orders and her physical presence.

Many of the men had either experienced her wrath or heard the stories surrounding the torture of those who opposed her. The promise for following her was a life better than they ever knew in the jungle and safety for their families left behind. Not bowing to her demands meant certain death to them and a life of slavery for the survivors. Only those in her inner circle, those older men gathered with her now in the barn were aware of what motivated her. Her father, Hector hated the American they were now hunting, hatred he taught Angelina from the time she was snatched from the coward. Angelina was a good student.

Angelina was dressed in a flowing red summer dress decorated with images of tropical flowers. Her crow black hair was pulled back off her face. Drawn back, it revealed the scars from burns down the left side of her face and shoulders. The hair was gone from behind her ear which itself was fastened to the side of her head with a diamond stud keeping it from sliding down. With her arms bared, the scars on her arm were clear. From her shoulder to her wrist her left arm looked more like melted plastic than skin. To view her from the opposite side was to see a beautiful Latin woman. To see her on the left was to see a woman who carried the scars of hatred and war.

Angelina began laying out the plans for the day. She recited the plans without notes or emotion. Each team was picked for their ability and task. The teams also knew failure was not an option if they wanted to return home when this was over. She pointed to each man, called him by a name she gave them on the spot and when their assignment was given, she ordered them out of her sight.

When Angelina finished dismissing almost everyone the only ones remaining in the barn was the same group of men she met with last night. She instructed each one again. The priest was hers to deal with, all the others were to be dealt with by the assignments just dispensed. When it was over, if she did not survive, they were to retrieve her body at all cost and take it back to where her father was hiding. Each of these selected knew, they had the hardest task of all. To return with her body to Hector was to signal failure to him. That wasn't an option either.

Chapter 82

Angelina left the men and returned to a small pop up camper outside the barn. She removed the dress and worked her way into a flight suit and boots. When finished, she made a strong cup of coffee ground from beans she brought with her. She let the steam from the coffee form a veil between her and the view she had of the rising sun over the corn field.

The field sparkled with the morning's dew. The sun, low behind the few trees at the end of the field, cast long morning shadows across the runway and the plane. She is happy. Today is going to be the completion of revenge and retribution on the man that disfigured her as a child and sent her father to prison.

Angelina began speaking to the field as if the man she was taught to hate was standing in front of her.

"My father told me how you stole my mother's affection away from him. When my father tried to free her and the village, you turned your Marines on my father and his workers. I know my father is not an innocent man but even a business man like father would not hold a baby over flames, bargaining for his life. But, today, you will get another chance to bargain, only this time you will look me in the eyes and fail."

Angelina began reviewing all that she had planned and the number of people she worked into her puzzle. Unlike most puzzles, Angelina's became clearer with each piece that was taken away. Still talking to the fields,

"Dan Faraday, the weak marshal who traded his loyalty for cash. Without him, we could not find Fr. Francis. Without Faraday, we would not have been able to fool Francis all these years that he was satisfying his conscience by supporting a baby he felt guilty over. Faraday was now out of the way.

Bill Colestock, he was the easiest to get to. It is so easy to manipulate a man who wants a woman he cannot have. Give him the opportunity and the means, he becomes your slave All we had to do was convince him that arranging for the poison with the flowers was all he must do to have the pretty Medical Examiner all to himself. With the priest and the sheriff out of the way, he would be able to pursue the Medical Examiner.

The girl that took my place. She had a good life. She thought she was off to a new life in America. But like others, her usefulness was gone. My men are good. She died without leaving any trace of who she really was. And the priest friend Fr. Steve, he was another weak man and easy to handle. Every holy man has something he doesn't want anyone else to know. It only took one phone call to him and he caved under the threat. What do I care that he was a priest? The devil and I will enjoy his company"

Angelina swirled the last bit of coffee in her cup and looked at it as if it had a message for her then threw the cup and all to the ground. A man dressed in a yellow flowered shirt and straw hat watched all of Angelina's actions. When she stepped back in her pop-up he followed her moves with thirsty eyes. He lit the stump of a cigar he was chewing without ever taking his eyes off her. Once lit he reached over took her hand, kissed it and then walked her to the barn.

Chapter 83

Susan woke up in a hotel room. Alone. She had no recollection of the night before. She was still dressed in the clothes she went out in last night. The space beside her in bed obviously wasn't used. Her mouth felt like her tongue was glued to the roof of her mouth and she was breaking into a cold sweat both from fear of how she got there and too much alcohol in her stomach.

She sheepishly put one foot on the floor and pushed herself slowly up from the bed. Catching sight of herself in the mirror, her hair was anything but perfect and her once crisp blouse was now a show of wrinkles. The message button on the room phone flashed and she pressed it.

"Good morning Susan, this is Bob. I hope you are feeling okay this morning. You were not feeling good last night when we arrived at the hotel. I thought it was best to get you a room and preserve your reputation as mayor. I had to leave early this morning for some work out of town, but we might be able to meet later tonight."

Susan felt a little better about the situation after listening to Bob's message. Now she just had to leave the hotel with some dignity and get herself ready for Fr. Steve's funeral.

Chapter 84

Michelle was up early and already running over in her head all that she discussed with Susan and Bob last night. Bob seemed like a nice enough man, but he kept eyeing her whenever Susan was not looking. The way he looked at her made her uncomfortable. It was not the same way he looked at Susan. She was worried for Susan, even though she didn't like her, but to leave with a man like that was dangerous for any woman.

Michelle still needed to get August the report on the fingerprints. But, the odds of him even giving her the time of day after last night was slim. However, he needed to know. The idea that Bill Colestock was involved in all of this was hard for her to stomach. The guy had always seemed so nice to her, even often going out of his way to make her feel comfortable. Now it made sense how he turned on her the other day. It will be even harder for August to accept.

She had already made repeated calls to his house with no answer. Most likely he was out-right avoiding her. She would see him at the funeral and tell him then. She decided to shower and make herself as attractive as she could today. Maybe August would give her a second chance. If not, there was always California to fall back on.

Stepping into the shower, Michelle didn't hear the latch on her apartment door open. The intruder sat down at her table and waited for her to come out of the shower.

Chapter 85

August was out of the house before the sun came up. He enjoyed the walk back up to the Courthouse to get his jeep. The cool morning air and the silence of the morning is what he needed after last night. The events of the week seemed to be more part of a day than a week with each day just slipping into another. When he arrived at the Courthouse, August didn't bother to go into the office, instead he went right to the jeep and headed out of town by way of the View Café. He recognized a few of the cars parked there. He was tempted to stop in and say hi, but that didn't work out so well last night.

He was a couple miles down a gravel county road before he decided to pull off on a pasture entrance. He sat there just off the road convincing himself that he made the right decision to skip Fr. Steve's funeral. After all, he should be mad at him for trying to bring up old memories that clearly Steve knew haunted him. He wished Demetrius was here right now. Even though he was part of all of this, he needed his reassurance that he was doing the right thing.

August pulled the jeep farther into the field to avoid any passing cars. He didn't want to be found today. While he was pouring coffee from the thermos, he didn't notice in his rear-view mirror, the line of SUV's that passed on the road on their way out to the main highway.

Chapter 86

Saine pulled a chair up to Michelle's kitchen table and helped himself to a cup of coffee. Dressed in the same clothes he wore last night, he sat back and started to thumb through the morning's paper making himself at home. He could hear the shower running and pictured the shapely figure of Michelle in the shower. No time for that now. He gave himself the liberty of checking the caller ID on her home phone. She'd made several calls already this morning. Three calls to the Sheriff and most likely they were about him. Content with that information he waited for Michelle to finish her shower.

Chapter 87

Angelina walked around her plane giving it a careful preflight inspection. The morning was starting to warm up quickly and there was little wind to contend with. She checked the windsock on the barn and it hung limp and she smiled. Everything was falling into place as it should. By the end of the day she would either successful in her mission or dead. Either way, she will have confronted the man who tried to destroy her family and made her a freak. He will know what it is like to see those he cares about tortured and killed. Angelina checked the payload to make sure it would function as promised.

Satisfied that it was what she wanted, she walked back to the barn to complete the final details of today's mission.

Chapter 88

Susan made it back to her office with only a few people noticing her exit from the hotel. She called Anna earlier to come into work to run errands for her and to provide some cover for her. The Courthouse was quiet as most people were not at work yet.

"Good morning Aunt Susan, I mean Madam Mayor. How are you this morning? You look very nice. Is that what you are wearing to Fr. Steve's funeral?"

Susan was a little taken back by the question. It was phrased more as an opinion on what she was wearing rather than a question. Susan immediately came back with,

"No, I was dressed for an early morning meeting and I will be changing before the funeral. Go across the street and get me some coffee. When you come back, make sure you knock before you come in. I need to make an important call."

Once Susan was sure that Anna was out of the office, she sat down at her desk and pulled Fr. Steve's phone out from her locked desk. Something had been bugging her about Steve's phone and she realized what it was this morning.

There was one number on the phone that she recognized. Comparing it with her own call record her suspicion was confirmed, it was the same number she used to try and retrieve information from the FBI. Why would Steve be calling the FBI the day he died? There was another number that she knew well. It was Bill's over at the diner, but it was Bill calling Fr. Steve. Those two had nothing in common that she could figure out. What was going on in her town? Another number was very strange. It had an exchange that Susan didn't recognize at all. She figured what the heck she pressed the return. She waited through four or five rings and was just about to hang up when it went to voice mail. A woman's voice heavy with an accent was on the recording. Susan clicked the phone off. Now even more puzzled. She didn't like this.

Once the funeral was over, she and August were going to get this settled. Susan placed it back in her drawer and locked it just as Anna knocked on the door with the coffee. Susan met her at the door, grabbed the coffee out of her hands with not even a thank you and walked out of the office.

Chapter 89

Michelle stopped dead as she walked down the hall from the bathroom. Saine jumped up from his chair. Michelle went to scream, not for help but at him. She felt somewhat familiar with him, but her instincts immediately told her his visit would lead to no good.

Knowing what was going to happen, Saine reached her in only a few steps and had his hand over her mouth but not in an aggressive manner, more like trying to quiet someone who was about to spoil a surprise party. Michelle slowly dropped her guard.

"Michelle, don't scream. I am not going to hurt you. But you need to listen carefully to me and don't try to make sense of what I am going to tell you. You can't leave this apartment today."

Saine's first mistake was trying to tell Michelle what to do.

"Who are you to order me? I am going to Fr. Steve's funeral, you know that from our time with Susan last night."

"Michelle, you are not listening to me. You will not leave this apartment. If you have any feelings for the Sheriff, and I know you do, you will not leave here."

"I don't understand. Who are you really?"

"I can't share that with you right now. There are things I need to do that hopefully will protect your community and those you are fond of. That is all I can tell you. Stay here. Give me your word."

Saine gave Michelle a story that seemed so impossible. She had every reason to doubt him.

"Because you saved my life I am supposed to believe you. Give me a good reason why I should."

"Because I might be the one that determines if August lives or dies today, it's that simple. Don't bother to look for your car keys, I have them, along with your gun. All you need to know is that I am doing this for you, August and mostly for myself. Do not leave."

With that, Saine walked out the door. Once on street level, he flattened the tires on Michelle's car and pitched the keys into the nearby bushes.

Chapter 90

August sat in the jeep fighting off the occasional grasshoppers and bees coming through the open windows. The coffee was gone, and the sun was starting to make it unbearable to stay in the jeep. All he needed to do was stay out here another hour and it would be too late to attend the funeral. He would have an excuse which no one could argue with.

The pastor from the next parish over, who often worked with Fr. Steve, would be resourceful enough to fill in.

August stepped out of the jeep and walked to the front to relieve himself of some of the coffee. He heard the drone of an airplane engine warming up and props cutting through the now thick morning air.

There was no reason for a plane to be in the next field. August was familiar with every crop dusting service in the area and the closest one was miles away. He climbed back in the jeep, flicked a grasshopper off the steering wheel and backed around in the field and headed out to the main road. Making a left on the gravel road he trolled cautiously up the road as if he was moving up the river in his boat on one of his duck hunting trips. The gravel creaked under the weight of the tires as they moved over the rocks.

A blast of July air blew into the window and August thought he could detect a hint of rain in the wind. When he reached a clearing in the cornfield he caught sight of the noise maker and a barn to his right with a windsock hanging from a pole at the highest peak. The twin prop plane, larger than most dusters in the area appeared to be rigged for a day of dusting. August decided to introduce himself to what was obviously a new business that opened without his knowledge. This visit would give him the real excuse he was looking for to avoid town.

As August drove through the field to the barn the plane made its final run down the makeshift runway and lifted into the wind. Not a problem, he would go ahead into the barn. Surely there would be someone around, these operations rarely worked without a ground crew.

August parked the jeep alongside the barn. Before turning it off he watched the plane bank over the field and wished he was up there with whoever it was piloting the duster. August pulled the latch up on the barn door and pulled the door towards him. The morning sun was hot on his back as the cool air still trapped in the barn rushed to get past him. His figure cast a shadow into the barn as the sun acted like a theater spotlight following him. Dust drifted through the sun beams turning to flecks of gold as they passed through. What the sun targeted he was not prepared for.

Chapter 91

August figured he would find some oily mechanic working on airplane parts, instead he found a full-size piece of plywood sitting on two sawhorses. Rising from the makeshift table was a scale model of Watercreek. Each building of the downtown was recreated in perfect detail as if it was someone's model railroad display. The Courthouse was in the center with all the buildings up and down Main Street each one spaced perfectly to scale.

Tacked to the wall behind the table was a map of Watercreek along with satellite views and tradition topographical maps. The Courthouse, the bank across the street as well as each business closest to the Courthouse on main street were marked with what looked like some type of barcodes like you would find on a product for sale. Next to the maps were pictures of August, Michelle, Susan, Bill from the diner and many other individuals who worked in the downtown region. Many looked as if they were taken with cameras at eye level obviously without the subject's knowledge.

There were also pictures of Fr. Steve, the girl who was with Steve and Dan Faraday. Those three, had X's through them. August was picking up the smell of something that was familiar to him from many years ago, the aroma of coffee that could only come from the jungles of his mission days. It was also the same coffee that Hector would drink when he was "entertaining" in the village. Another even more disturbing smell. The rank cigar and body odor followed by the sulfur smell of rotten eggs.

August was locked in place. Whispering,

"He's here."

August reached for the reassurance of his Glock .45 and pulled it out. Stepping back outside, he walked to where he originally saw the plane preparing for take-off. Laying on the ground just beyond the tire tracks of the plane was a cell phone. Still active August picked it up and pulled up the call history. Five minutes ago, a call from Fr. Steve's number was recorded.

August went cold in the July heat.

Chapter 92

Once August recovered from the shock he turned around saw what was originally hidden by the plane was now clear, barrels of diesel fuel and oil, the makings of homemade napalm.

They were all empty.

August knew this was the start of a day he always feared. It was all coming together the events of the week, the insistence on Steve's part to get Angelina the disappearance of Dan and the visit in the hospital by Angelina. August's chest tightened. He dropped to his knees wincing through the pain.

"Just give me one more day. This is my fight to finish not yours."

Chapter 93

August, breathing like a marathoner after a run stumbled to the jeep. He crawled into the seat and threw the handgun on the passenger seat. Spinning the jeep around cutting ruts into the grass, he headed toward town and drove as fast as the gravel road would allow. Turning on the main highway, he activated the siren and lights and at the same time called Michelle's number. Michelle's number rang three times and then went to voice mail. August disconnected and pitched it on the seat beside him.

By the time August reached Watercreek, it was almost 10:00 and the bells of the church were ringing calling for the start of Fr. Steve's funeral Mass. Everything seemed normal as he made his way down the main street. The old guys were at their post in the shade of the big maple tree on the lawn. While he was stopped at the light, he could see George speaking more with his hands. Probably embroiled in some political dissertation. Bill was unwinding the awning over the diner to protect the windows from the sun. The farmers were pulling away from the main street and heading back out on the main highway to their farms.

August thought the town was too quiet. So quiet he felt as if he was driving around in the model he just left. Quiet was hanging like a foreboding thunderstorm.

August parked and ran into his office. Pulling up his radio, he called the main dispatch of the state police. Then August heard the drone of a plane. The sound was too low for a plane over this part of town. Running out of the office he looked to the sound and saw the same plane he witnessed earlier now flying low over town heading south. The plane made a steep bank as it neared the end of the highway stretch and came back around flying lower than the first pass. August could see the guys on the Courthouse lawn stand to find the plane in the sky. Bill stepped out from under the awning and shielded his eyes while he looked to the sky. As the plane came closer to downtown, August could see a liquid trailing from it dropping down over the town. The fluid sparkled like rain. Rainbows appeared in the wake as the sun cut through.

As the plane passed over, the fluid drenched every person, building and creature in its path. The smell of diesel fuel filled the air and people reacted in disgust at what was an apparent misdirected dump of fuel by the plane. As soon as the plane made its pass, charges were launched from the roof tops of the buildings August saw marked on the maps.

Canisters of flames dropped to the streets igniting everything and everybody that was touched by the liquid. A launch from the top of the bank building next to Bill's diner landed on top of a car parked in front of the Courthouse. Immediately the car burst into flames. In rapid succession cars began to explode as flames from one reached out to another like a violent game of tag. People ran, becoming human torches trying to escape the flames that chased them faster. No one could get close to another without bursting into flames themselves. Buildings began to ignite and burn. Within seconds, the entire downtown was rolling flames and black smoke. Glass was shattering as store windows popped from the heat.

The heat hit August with the force of fire seeking air and more fuel. The roar was more intense than any tornado winds. Screams for help started to rise above the roar. The men on the lawn laid across one another dead but still displaying a desperate attempt to save each other. Bill had retreated to his diner but was now trapped inside by a car which exploded and landed at the only exit. August could see the diner sucking the flames in and spitting them out the top windows. August could only see one way out of the furnace and that was to run through the flames to the other side of the highway which seemed untouched by the spray and flames. Grabbing a shotgun from the locker in his office, checking for shells in the chamber, August ran from the Courthouse, through the flames which were starting to burn off on the sidewalk and made it to the other side.

What wasn't on fire was black from the charring. August chest tightened bending him in half as he reached the other side of the highway. The bells continued to ring at St. Mary's. No one there was aware of what was happening to their town.

Turning to find a clear spot in the carnage, August heard the plane on a return loop. This time it made a direct line toward the church. August knew exactly what was happening, an attack on the church would hit all the leading members of the community including his closest friends. He was supposed to be there. In sudden clarity Demetrius's words came back to him. He was called to be a priest, not for what he had done, but for what he was expected to do. He didn't fire on Hector when he had the chance. That was his failure. Now, he could not fail again to protect the people he was placed to guard. He knew what he had to do and who was here to face him. He had escaped this devil for years.

"It is my necessary sin."

Today, he and the devil would both either walk into hell together, or he would be free to live the life he was called to.

Fire sirens began wailing over the city as volunteers raced to the two stations in town. Screams and shouts muffled by the winds and firestorm created a horrific symphony of sounds. August turned in the direction of the church and saw a plume of smoke rise over the trees. It was evident the church was suffering the same fate as the center of town. August could only be in one place. Again, he was torn between duty and desire.

Michelle was surely in the church, but his role was here with what was in front of him. Michelle would be one more suffering the fate of knowing him.

Chapter 94

Michelle sat at her table. She didn't know how to process all the information from Saine. All she was sure of was that she needed to reach August before any of Saine's predictions came true.

Michelle heard a plane very low followed by muffled explosions. She looked out her north window towards downtown. Heavy smoke was billowing up. The smoke, a mixture of black and white from the fires that were being hit by water and gray from the burning of the old wood and other building materials. She knew she was too late to warn August, he was either dead, or in the thick of all she saw.

Before leaving, Saine barricaded the door with a free-standing chest in the hall of the apartment. With several good tries, Michelle pushed it away from the door enough to let her small frame out. She figured Saine knew she would get out. He was only trying to slow her down. This small gesture on his part is what helped her to believe what he shared. He could have killed her or tied her to something in the apartment. Racing through the halls of the apartment building she started replaying the new information from Saine. It was hard to believe what Saine told her about being an undercover marshal investigating numerous breeches of the witness protection program. To do this, he had to assume a new identity and operate completely outside the marshal division. Saine was tasked with finding the leak that had exposed so many and that would ultimately lead to a confrontation in Watercreek.

Saine tracked the leak of August's identity to Dan Faraday. He worked his way into the Omaha office as a new agent. This gave him the opportunity to watch Faraday and understand the network he developed. Faraday's reach was extensive and was funded with payoffs and bonuses by the Fuentes. Saine was in the process of reporting in his findings when Faraday's car exploded right in front of him. That is when he knew that things were heading in the direction of August. Hector has a habit of eliminating those who work for him when he's finished with them. Saine new this lesson all too well. That is why he needed to be so careful. He was close to ending the flood of information.

According to Saine, the woman behind the attack that will happen soon is supposedly Hector's daughter. The woman who was killed in the car wreck was an imposter sent to test Fr. Steve's loyalty. Dan Faraday turned Steve against August by blackmailing him over an incident earlier in Steve's priesthood. Steve was to pick up the girl and bring her to August. The Fuentes believed that if she was in town, August would never leave, and they would be able to achieve their goal of killing him in his own town. But then, Fr. Steve could not be trusted. He made a call to the FBI right before picking up the Angelina replacement. This was shared with the Fuentes who have contacts deep in all agencies. That is why Fr. Steve and the girl never made it back to Watercreek.

Saine left Michelle's apartment before completing all the information. Michelle now understood the complete destruction of the corpses in her care. With the corpses destroyed, there was no way to collaborate Saine's theory. These people are obviously very dangerous.

When Michelle finally reached street level, the smell of the fumes coming from the town center only blocks away almost consumed her. She started running towards the heavy smoke, stopping many times to catch her breath in the acid air. She had to reach August, before he encountered Saine. Without knowing what she knew, August will most likely kill him on sight thinking he orchestrated the attack.

Chapter 95

Angelina landed the twin engine plane back on the makeshift runway. The plane was noticeably lighter now that the payload was dumped on the targets. Angelina and her copilot walked side by side back to the barn. As they walked, Angelina worked a small .32 caliber revolver out of the pocket of her flight suit. As her copilot paced a short distance in front of her, she pulled the .32 up to the back of his head and fired one clean shot. He dropped to the ground in front of her.

In the barn Angelina stripped the flight suit off and tossed it in a corner of the barn. Walking to the back corner, she uncovered a motorcycle loaded for her with a radio and weapons. As she pulled around the edge of the barn, she set fire to the corner of the building. Pulling away she watched in her mirror the flames rising around the barn and smoke going straight up in the windless air. Fire which had so horribly disfigured her, was now going to be the vehicle which set her free and enacted her revenge.

Chapter 96

Susan looked back at the building that was once St. Mary's church. She was outside on her cell when the plane flew over and flares dropped on the roof. The explosion that followed the fly over of the plane incinerated the roof of the old church and sent debris flying out over the parking lot.

Susan could hear the screams coming from inside the church and watched helpless as people ran out of the building. Most coming out were covered in building materials and blood. She turned toward the center of town and could see thick black smoke rising. She knew her town was in trouble and with the attack on the church, she was sure it was connected to August and Fr. Steve in some way.

Trying to drive her car was pointless. The debris blocked the exit of the lot and those that could get out had already congested the narrow road. Susan started to walk down the hill to the center of town. Repeatedly she tried calling emergency services to find out what was happening. No one was answering. She could hear fire trucks and other sirens responding. None were coming towards the church. She knew she should stay and help but she believed she could be of more value in town. She chastised herself for thinking of the political gain she would receive being visible in town, but she quickly convinced herself that was part of being a politician.

Halfway to town a volunteer fireman recognized her and picked her up. He had no information for her other than they were all called to drop what they were doing and respond. The best he knew there was some sort of attack on the city. They reached the edge of the business district just across from the Courthouse. The fireman gave Susan an extra turnout coat. Much too big for her but she thought it gave her an air of authority.

Standing just outside of the burning zone, she began to cry as she looked at her downtown now unrecognizable as anything more than a massive bonfire. The Courthouse itself was blackened. All the trees surrounding it were black twigs standing in sorrow. The hotel where she had just spent the night was showing the effects of the intense heat. Canopies and signs were melted or gone and every car in the parking lot was on fire or burned out.

Chapter 97

August made his way back into his office. He broke open the cabinet containing a variety of shotguns and assault rifles. When he took over the office he never imagined using one of them, let alone having enough manpower to match all the weapons the rack contained. Now he grabbed as many as he could with the plan of passing out the weapons to the first citizens he came across.

Stepping out the front entrance of the Courthouse, August was met with a scene out of his nightmares. The roar of the flames was doing little to drown the screams coming from up and down the main street. The sky which was already steely gray from the approaching storm was now black from the layer of smoke rolling up from the buildings. People were trapped on either side by the wall of flames that now cut the city in half.

August caught sight of Stan Farney pulling up. Stan jumped from his truck dressed in his fire turnout gear. August hollered,

"Stan, get up here."

Stan following the orders from August, left the door of his pickup standing open and sprinted across the Courthouse lawn. Before he could make it half way across the lawn, he was picked off by a shot out of nowhere. August pulled back into the Courthouse door frame and tried to spot the shooter. August ran back through the Courthouse to the other side. Coming out the opposite side of the building put him on the highway side. It didn't take long to see where the shot came from.

A shooter was standing on the corner ready to take another shot. August leveled the shotgun in his direction knowing full well he was out of range.

The shot had the effect August hoped for. The shooter turned towards August positioned behind the solid walls of the doorway. August knew what was coming next. A hail of bullets riddled the side of the building as August laid on his belly protecting his head from the shower of mortar and bricks being knocked loose. When the shooting stopped, August moved through the Courthouse on his belly back to the main street side. Smoke hung a few feet above his head. The emergency lights flashed through the smoke showing up as pockets of white and red light.

A caravan of dusty SUVs lined the highway. Men dressed in jungle camouflage uniforms were positioned all along as a wall to prevent anyone from moving out of the area. August pulled himself upright with the help of a door frame into Susan office. He moved into her office which gave him a north and west view of downtown. Stan was laying out on the lawn. August felt certain he was dead, but he needed to try and help him. August grabbed a statue off Susan's desk and threw it through the window. The minute he tried to get through the window another rain of gunfire shattered all the other windows.

The bullets passed through and riddled the opposite wall knocking pictures and political collections to the floor. August took refuge behind Susan's heavy desk. Another volley of bullets ripped through the office. August moved to the outside wall for protection. A surge of bullets tore apart the Mayor's desk like it was made of cardboard. The drawer of the desk dropped out spilling the contents in front of August.

Laying among the contents on the floor, was Fr. Steve's phone. For a moment August forgot about the attack that was raging around him. He reached for the phone. What was Susan doing with the phone and better yet, how did she get her hands on it? August stroked the phone as if it was a precious object, something that should be revered. August used Steve's phone often enough on hunting and fishing trips. It was nothing for him to tap in the access code.

Once in he went through the call list. He found the call Steve made just before the wreck. He also found a call to a number he recognized as the FBI office in Kansas City. Why would Steve be contacting the FBI? There were numerous other calls that August couldn't identify with numbers that looked like they were out of the country. The number that finally sent a chill through August was the number for Dan Faraday. Steve called Dan the day of the accident. According to his knew handler, Dan was killed on the day after Steve died. August sat in the middle of the rubble that was Susan's office.

With his back against the wall facing his attackers he was safe for the moment. A third barrage of gunfire brought him back to the present. Hugging the wall for cover he slid over to the door to the office and back out into the main hallway.

Chapter 98

All went quiet, the calm before a storm people always talk about. Someone must have commanded the shooters to stand down. August raised himself cautiously against the door facing the main part of downtown. Walking up the steps towards him was the image of the beautiful woman he last saw in his hospital room.

August watched as she moved with confidence towards the Courthouse doors. He suddenly realized what a fool he had been. Here was the reflection of the woman he watched burn and Hector assassinate. The figure walking towards him was more beautiful than her mother and with more confidence than she ever possessed. He thought maybe he was already dead and this was some ugly after life. She walked toward him like a confident runway model, her eyes locked on August. When she came close enough he could finally look in to her eyes, the haunting feeling of talking to Balifour came again. The woman had no soul. She was a walking shell of Hectors evil. It was hard to believe these were the same eyes that locked on him years ago. The disfigurement of her face and arm. The burned baby smoldering in the puddle.

Angelina.

August moved to get a better view but also to stay covered by the heavy stone of the building. He could tell it was her that commanded the silence of the guns. The smoke of the fires seemed to fall behind her in obedience. After a few seconds August stepped out from cover feeling like he was safe from attack.

As August stepped to the front step of the entrance Angelina raised her hand as a signal for all to hold their fire. August walked slowly toward her, never moving his gaze. She was the embodiment of her mother and more.

Focused on her, he failed to notice the man walking up behind her. As they drew closer the view behind her continued to block August from looking any further. When she was only steps away from him, she took one step aside to reveal the partner behind her.

Hector Fuentes greeted August with a sadistic smile and a gun pointed directly at August.

"It is good to see you Captain Father. I never expected to see you again. I have been truly blessed."

The sarcasm of Hector was enough to start the pounding of revenge in August head. He ignored the pain swelling in his chest.

"What do you want Hector?"

"All I want is your soul priest. I have a debt to deliver you. The fact that you are now a lawman makes it even easier. You stole my Galina from me with the thoughts you planted in her head and you tried to steal Angelina. You are the cause my daughter carries these scars. Now I want you to burn as you should have that night along with your Marines. And priest, I want you to know, your parents did not stand in my way. The same way I crushed them, is the way I will crush you. Your father was such a weak man. Just like you he hesitated and for that he died. The men in your family must all be cowards."

August felt the life drain from him as he stared at Hector but did not see him. It was as if at this moment, he was the only person on the Courthouse steps. Hector began to walk closer to August, it was then that August turned to Angelina. August dropping his gun to his side,

"It appears the man that calls himself your father and I have more than one score to settle. Since I am most likely going to die today, let me tell you what really happened. Then you and the man you think is your father can do with me what you want.

I can see how you can believe his lies. The man you call father is apparently still a powerful man capable of creating any environment for you that fits his needs. But you have two other people in your life that cared even more for you than this man ever did. You were nothing more than his prize race horse, his trophy from one more village. Your mother and the man that loved you, your real father were hard working people in the village where you were born. Hector enslaved many of the men in the village with

215

loans and other obligations which they would never be able to pay back. Christian, your father worked for Hector to protect your mother, you and your brother.

You probably didn't even know you had a brother, did you? As a result, your parents were poor, but honest people. Your mother, a woman looking just like you was the most beautiful woman in the area. No other woman came close to her beauty or determination. Hector was always jealous that a simple man like Christian was so respected and had a woman that he could never have. Hector tricked your father into working for him most of his life. His only goal was to distract your father while he had his way with your mother.

Your mother confided in me as her priest the things Hector did to her and required of her. Your mother was raped repeatedly by Hector. To cover his actions, Hector raided your parent's village in the jungle. He claimed he was looking for a traitor that had turned him into the government. My sin is that I was not strong enough at the time to save either you or your mother. I watched Hector execute your mother. When I tried to shoot him, I failed. He came at me with his knife."

August pulled up his shirt,

"Here, this is the scar I received when I rolled to protect you from him. He snatched you from me and threw you over like you would throw a stray cat to the side of the road. You landed in ruins of a burning hut. I was knocked out by Hector when we fought. When I came to, all the Marines were dead. You were laying in the smoldering remains of a hut. Christian, your real father, came back for you. He took you away under the orders of Hector. I learned later, Hector murdered him. He tortured Christian and finally killed him only after he told your father what he had been doing to your mother. I believe Christian thought that if he took you with him to Hector as he ordered, maybe you would have a better life than what was left in the village.

Your brother, who he also stole was never heard from again. It wasn't long, and a Marine medivac helicopter landed. I was taken away and placed in a hospital. It was made clear to me that Hector meant to finish the job, so the government hid me for my protection and those around me. Apparently, Hector counted on you carrying out your own revenge based on his distorted stories."

Angelina turned toward Hector. Hector could tell that the rage he had instilled in Angelina was now turning against him. Angelina raised her weapon and pointed it at Hector.

"Tell me the truth now old man!" Hector just shrugged his shoulders in a display of cockiness. Laughing while he talked,

"What the priest tells you is true. Your mother was nothing more to me than my whore. Your father, was a gutless man. He cried and prayed to Jesus like a little boy when I killed him. I knew you would be valuable to me someday...and see you are."

Immediately Angelina saw him for his lies. The rage for being duped all these years overpowered her. Angelina pulled the trigger. Hector, anticipating her action ducked and fired his weapon. Angelina's bullet missed Hector.

Susan, was walking up behind Hector, not realizing what was taking place between these strangers in her town. The bullet from Angelina's gun struck Susan just below her rib cage. She was blown back down the steps, blood leaking from her back. Hector's aim was better. He hit Angelina, his intended target. She fell to her knees not fully comprehending what placed her there. She was looking at the man who for twenty years she admired and called father. Now he was her killer. August, reached for his shotgun on the ground. In the next second, he was brought down by a bullet from Hector. The bullet caught August in his right shoulder forcing him to drop the shotgun.

Chapter 99

Saine worked his way through the chaos of the burning town to his hotel room. No one was left in the hotel. With the elevators locked he was slightly out of breath from running the flights of stairs to his room. Once inside he slid a large duffle from under his bed. Placing it on the bed he reached in and pulled a rifle already scoped and sighted in.

Saine pulled the scope up and looked out the window to the burning town. Smoke swirled in small funnels as the draft from the heat formed multiple fire tornados. He could see the action taking place on the Courthouse lawn. Saine took the butt of his handgun and broke out the window. He pulled binoculars from the duffle and stepped backed to the window.

Through the smoke he could see Susan laying on the sidewalk at the base of the steps still in the same clothes he saw her in last night. There was another woman stretched out on the upper sidewalk. The last time he saw her was as a severely burned baby. The man he knew as Hector Fuentes was pointing a gun at August. August had obviously been hit once already. He could see Hectors men coming out from hiding like ants drawn to a dropped piece of candy.

Saine placed the crosshairs of the scope on his target and squeezed the trigger. The bullet passed through Hector's neck as Saine chambered another round. Everyone took cover not knowing where the shot came from. Saine watched Hector's men scanning the roof tops for the shooter but the smoke was Saine's shield. Saine pulled out his cell and dialed a preset code and then returned to his sniper mission. It was becoming increasingly difficult to find targets through the smoke. Saine ran to other rooms and followed the same procedure breaking through windows and finding targets. Finally, his phone call paid off. The glass in the broken windows rattled as the drone of several helicopters hovered over the edge of the business district. Ropes dropped from the sky as Marines began repelling down.

It didn't take long for the Marines to out-number the oppositions on the ground. In a brief fire fight, the Marines killed or rounded up all the attackers. Other Marines were working with fire personnel and first responders to bring the fires under control. Saine stashed his weapons back in the duffle and removed any evidence of ever being in the room. He carried his duffle down the back stairs, avoiding contact with anyone. Working his way back through alleys on a planned route he met his ride at the far end of the main business district.

An old pickup took him north out of town as a flood of Marine transports, fire trucks and ambulances came from the opposite direction. Saine reached down in his shirt and tugged at a lanyard around his neck. Pulling it up the entire length he held a wooden cross, rounded on the edges from wear. Without the driver even noticing, he kissed the cross and to himself said,

"Now you can rest father. Watch over my sister."

He dropped the cross and the leather string into an envelope, scribbled August Hawk's name and address on it and handed it over to the driver.

Chapter 100

Michelle fought her way through the rubble to the Courthouse lawn. She was delayed by countless citizens who called out for aid. When she arrived at the Courthouse she could barely breathe from the smoke. Michelle found Susan. She was barely conscious. Michelle tried to stop the bleeding but knew it was already too late. Susan with a limp grip on Michelle's arm begged her to stop trying to save her.

"Get August," she mouthed to Michelle.

Michelle looked up the steps to see three people lying on the steps and walk. She could identify only August by his usual jeans and polo shirt. She left Susan on the walk and ran past a man and woman. The woman was the one that appeared at August bedside only days ago. The disfigured side of her face was facing the sky.

She reached August already trying to stop the bleeding himself. Forgetting about Susan, Michelle hugged August as he sat against the Courthouse wall. She could feel his blood seeping through her shirt. She kissed him lightly on his cheek as she moved her hand over his wound.

"What's happening August. Who are these people?"

August began to respond, but Michelle remembered Susan. She pulled August up using his good arm.

"Come with me. Susan has been shot, and she wants you."

August could only imagine. This woman had some explaining as to why she hid evidence from him. When they approached Susan, August felt a wave of satisfied revenge then guilt for even having the thought.

Susan, with little energy left motioned for August to come closer. She whispered in his ear. Michelle could only watch as the two had a private conversation in each other's ears. When finished, August traced the sign of the cross on her forehead and Michelle could hear him say,

"Your sins are forgiven, go in peace" as he gently laid her head down on the sidewalk.

Susan was gone.

August walked back up the steps past Hector whose blood was running down the Courthouse steps. Angelina was laying just above him on the sidewalk. August lifted Angelina's head and cradled it in his arms. He stroked her hair pulling it back behind her ear. He then rolled her over revealing to Michelle the beautiful woman she was. August held the baby in his arms that he tried to protect years ago.

A steady rain began to fall soon turning to a heavy down pour. August and Michelle sat on the sidewalk holding Angelina as the rain began to ease the fires and wash the blood down the steps. The woman who had been the source of so much destruction was now in the arms of someone who loved her but didn't know why.

August traced the cross on her forehead and with Michelle's help, carried her out of the rain.

Chapter 101

One Week Later

August and Michelle stepped out of a plane at the Buenos Aires airport. They waited as a coffin was carried off the plane and taken to a waiting hearse. The hearse, with August and Michelle following close behind in a mud caked Land Rover, snaked through backcountry roads. Their destination, Angelina's home village.

When they arrived, August was surprised to see how it was rebuilt from the days of destruction. The coffin of Angelina was carried into a small stone church where they were greeted by the local missionary priest.

When Mass finished, Angelina's coffin was carried back down the aisle of the church by men who were either cousins or uncles of Angelina. One of the cousins reminded August of the stranger in town Bob Saine, but he excused it as being a foolish thought.

Now that Hector was gone, the people in the village were no longer afraid to embrace their Angelina for who she really was. As the coffin passed August, he turned to Michelle who pulled from her bag the cross that occupied August kitchen drawer. August placed the cross on the coffin and watched as it was carried out the back door of the mission to the cemetery to be buried beside her mother and father.

Chapter 102

The Next Day

August and Michelle traveled together to the airport. It was a long four-hour ride spent in awkward silence for both. August wasn't sure if it was hotter and more humid here than he remembered or if it was just the nerves and lack of air conditioning in the Land Rover.

Michelle kept hoping that August would reach out and just touch her like he did back in the hospital. August wanted her. All the events of the past week seemed to have never happened with her sitting beside him. When the Rover pulled up to the airport, neither were anxious to step out. August finally came around and opened her door.

Walking into the concourse they looked like a typical tourist couple winding down after a long vacation. August gave Michelle a tight hug. He pulled her close and could feel the contours of her body, wishing to himself that he could hold onto her just a little longer. He hoped the smell of her perfume and the tightness of her body would never leave his memory.

Michelle kissed August hard on the lips, a vow that she made to herself that she was going to carry out. August allowed it to happen and even go on longer than it should, but he knew what had to be done. He gently pushed Michelle away and with no other words spoken since they left the village, he walked her to the gate.

Michelle checked in at the gate with August standing by her side holding her Marine backpack, the only piece of luggage she traveled with. She waved her ticket in August's direction, reached out and touched him on the shoulder and walked through the door to the tarmac and the waiting plane bound for California.

When the door closed behind her, August felt like his feet were glued to the floor. When he could finally move them, he walked slowly to his gate while fumbling for his passport.

"Can I help you sir," in English laced with a Latin accent.

"Yes, I should have a ticket waiting for me, Father, Francis Stratton."

On board the plane back to the United States, Francis settled into his seat, it felt cool after the days of jungle humidity. He watched out the window as workers loaded suitcases and others tended fuel and food trucks. The sun caused him to squint and made him a little sleepy, something he hadn't had much of a chance to do lately. He gave in to sleep.

Francis was startled awake by the pungent odor of cigar and body stench. He could see through the crack of the seat in front of him, a man with a wild tropical print shirt. Francis listened as the man's garbled voice called the attendant "sweetie" and ordered a shot of whiskey. When finished he turned and looked with one eye through the separation in seats. Francis made a half reach for a gun that wasn't there. Balifour's words drooled out of his mouth,

"Good morning Father, you enjoy the flight."